Remember Dippy

By
SHIRLEY REVA VERNICK

Remember Dippy

By
SHIRLEY REVA VERNICK

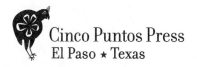

Cinco Puntos Press
El Paso ★ Texas

Remember Dippy
Copyright © 2013 by Shirley Reva Vernick

First Edition
10 9 8 7 6 5 4 3 2 1

Library of Congress Cataloging-in-Publication Data

Vernick, Shirley Reva.
  Remember Dippy / by Shirley Reva Vernick.—First edition.
    pages cm
  Summary: While reluctantly agreeing to help out with his autistic older cousin during the last summer before high school, Johnny discovers a new friend in his cousin, as well as an appreciation for what really matters in a person.
ISBN 978-1-935955-48-1 (Hardback); ISBN 978-1-935955-58-0 (Paper); E-ISBN 978-1-935955-49-8
[1. Cousins—Fiction. 2. Autism—Fiction. 3. Friendship—Fiction.] I. Title.

  PZ7.V5974Re 2013
  [Fic]--dc23
                    2012043174

Book and cover design by Anne M. Giangiulio
Layout by the House Compositor: she's learning from the best!
Thanks to Richard Horak for his heroic help with the cover.

For Annie and Zoe

Chapter 1

Hull, Vermont, should be named Dull, Vermont. More cows than houses. No mall, no roller rink, not even a mini-putt. So I knew my thirteenth summer was going to be a boring one like all the others. What I didn't know was that it was going to be a rotten summer. My mother didn't drop the bomb until I got home after the last day of school.

Mom was making her famous black-cherry iced tea when I strolled into the kitchen at quarter past three. "Hi," I said with my nose already in the 'fridge. I grabbed a pint of fudge ripple, snatched a spoon off the drying rack, and dove in.

"Hey Johnny, happy summer vacation," she said. "When you come up for air, I've got some good news."

"What's up?" I asked, hopping up on the counter.

"I got a new client this week. A big one."

"Sweet," I said. Mom is an interior decorator, and since she and Dad split two years ago, she's really been trying to amp up her business. "Whose house?"

"Not a house." She stirred the iced tea hard, like she was nervous or something. "It's not a house and, well, it's not around here. It's a museum, an entire museum, in Upstate New York. I'll need to go there. Be there. Most of the summer probably."

"New York? We're going to New York—as in, a real city with real things to do?"

"Not us, Johnny. Me. It wouldn't work for you to— "

My chest clamped. "So you're shipping me off to Dad's." My father lives in Northern Maine now, a nothing place like Hull except that I don't have any friends there. And ever since my father met his girlfriend Kim, it's not much fun when I visit—which isn't very often.

"No, don't worry," Mom said. "Your dad isn't even available. He's going on a cruise next month, remember? You'll stay with my sister."

I felt myself start to relax. Aunt Collette is awesome, plus she's local, not to mention that she manages the 7-11, where slushies are on the house for family. Mom could do her thing all summer, and I could do mine. A perfect plan.

Or so I thought.

"There's more good news, Johnny." She tried to smile, but she didn't really mean it, so it came out as a grimace. "I found you a job."

I plunged the spoon into the ice cream and raised an eyebrow. "What kind of job?"

"Helping out with your cousin."

"What?" I jumped off the counter.

"Just while Collette's at work, that's all. Then you're free."

"But Mom—"

"No buts. If you don't watch him, Collette will have to take in a college student from Burlington to do it, and then she won't have room for you, and then I won't be able to go to New York. It's the only way, Johnny. Now go pack. I'm dropping you off at five."

That is how the perfect plan turned into the perfect disaster.

Now, before you go thinking I'm a selfish brat, you've got to understand about my cousin Remember. Yes, that's right, his name is Remember—straight out of some New Age baby-naming book. He's two years older than me, and he's what polite people call different. I call him weird. He doesn't have friends. He looks the wrong way when you speak to him. He either talks a mile a minute or not at all. He's stubborn and high-strung. I could go on and on. Not that it's his fault. Mom says he's wired differently. Aunt Collette says he's just who he is. But fault or no fault, he's hard even to be around, much less look after. This was definitely going to be a disaster.

I trudged to my room and stuffed my clothes, GameCube, iPod, toothbrush, and the remains of a sack of Hershey's Kisses into my duffel bag. Then I wedged the bag and my bike into the car and waited for Mom, who was standing in the driveway talking with Mr. Boots, the cranky old man who lives in the other half of our duplex. At least I wouldn't have him nagging me to pipe down my music these next couple of months.

We drove in silence to my aunt's house at the bottom of a little dead end road. Mom parked on the street in front of the mailbox, which used to say THE DIPPY'S in those hardware store adhesive letters. But after last month's big rainstorm, it said T E DIPP, which inspired some kids to start calling my cousin The Dipp. I'm pretty sure he didn't notice, though. He doesn't really have anything to do with the other kids in town. He takes an extra early bus to a special school in Peak Landing, gets back late, and then he's mostly at home, except when he's hanging out at our house.

"All right," said Mom, turning off the engine. I hopped out and started unloading my stuff. When I finished, she was still sitting there, gripping the steering wheel.

"You coming in?" I asked through the open door.

"Look, Johnny, you are okay with this, right? I know this is sudden, and a whole summer is a long time..."

Sudden is right. Sudden and, if you ask me, unfair. But Mom needed—needed and wanted—this project bad, so I didn't really have a choice, did I, not unless I wanted to ruin her chance for the big time. "I'll cope," I said, although I wasn't sure I meant it.

Her face softened, and she finally let go of the wheel.

After I stashed my bike in the garage, we walked into the house without knocking. No one was in sight, but we could hear water running, and in a minute Aunt Collette bounced down the stairs, yanking her 7-11 shirt on over her tie-dye tank top and shaking her long dark hair into place. She's only a few years younger than Mom, but she looks a generation younger.

"Hello, sweetness!" Aunt Collette gripped my arms and kissed the top of my head. "That new punk I hired called in sick, so I've gotta cover for a while till Pete can get there. Dang, I hate the night shift." She pulled a tube of cherry-Popsicle colored lipstick out of her jeans and started applying a coat.

"Maybe you could hire me," I brightened. "Then you can be at home more." Working the 7-11 counter sounded a lot more fun, and way easier, than dealing with my cousin.

"Sorry, hon," she ruffled my hair. "We don't hire anyone under eighteen. But don't worry—I'll be back in time for *Reality Island*, and I'll bring a pizza home with me. How's that sound?"

Mom didn't look thrilled, but instead of protesting, she hugged me good-bye and reminded me to floss. "You still need to cut our grass every week," she added. "The mower's in the garage. Just ask Mr. Boots to let you in."

"I'll remind him," Aunt Collette said, walking Mom to the front door. "Johnny, make yourself at home while I walk your mother out. You've got the amethyst room."

All the rooms in my aunt's house are actually blue—except for the doorframes, which are painted

SHIRLEY REVA VERNICK

different colors, and she calls the rooms by that color, so you feel like you're living in the White House. Aunt Collette is quirky that way, but if it helps her deal with being a single parent to a weird son, I say go for it.

I carried my bag upstairs, plopped it next to the guest room bed, and considered myself officially settled in. The only thing left to do was say hi to the ferrets, who live on top of the spare dresser. Linguini and Jambalaya clucked at me and stuck their twitching noses through the cage slots. I gave them each a sliver of a Hershey's Kiss—chocolate is their favorite—and headed back downstairs.

"Now," said Aunt Collette when she came back inside, "all we need is Remember. Dang, where is that boy—Remember?"

Suddenly, the door to the entertainment center opened, and my cousin climbed out. "I'm here, Ma," he grinned. He's small for fifteen, but that cupboard must have been a tight squeeze even for him. He was crumpled from the top of his wavy brown hair to the bottom of his plaid shorts, and his skinny knees were pinched pink. "I was in my special place," he said, pushing his hair away from his forehead and pinning his owlish gray eyes on me. Something about him— the way he held himself, the big round eyes, the lack of cool—made him look younger than he was, as if he'd only borrowed his clothes from a real fifteen-year-old. "That's my special place."

"Well, your cousin doesn't know about special places, so please try to stay in view while I'm gone, okay?"

"Yup," he nodded.

"All right," she said slowly, like she wasn't convinced. "Johnny, you're in charge now. The store number's on the 'fridge. Help yourself to anything."

"We'll be fine," I told her, and I forced myself to smile. But what I was really thinking was that maybe Mom was right: a whole summer is a really long time.

Chapter 2

"So, Mem," I said once we were alone. I always call my cousin that. My aunt says when I was little and couldn't say my R's, I used to call him 'Memba, and from there it got shortened to Mem. "You want to help me unpack?"

"Nope." He plunked himself on the floor and turned on the TV.

Okay, no problem, I didn't really feel like unpacking anyway. Instead, I nabbed a bottle of bubbly water from the kitchen and joined Mem, who was watching *Jeopardy*. From the second I sprawled on the couch, he didn't take his eyes off my water bottle, so finally I asked if he wanted a drink.

"Do you want a drink?" he echoed, which is one of his more annoying habits. I used to think he was mocking me when he parroted my questions until I realized he does it to everyone sooner or later. "Want a drink?" he repeated and ran to the kitchen. He came back a minute later with a can of Dr. Pepper, which must have been his own hidden stash because I sure hadn't seen any sodas when I was nosing around the 'fridge.

I learned something about Mem while we watched the contestants butt brains: he can read. I was never sure what they taught him at that special school, but there he was, reading the answers right along with Alex Trebek. He didn't get any of the questions, but heck, neither did I. Oh, and another thing I learned about my cousin: he can belch like a truck driver.

There's not much else to tell about my first night. Aunt Collette got home around eight with a large pizza, as promised. I didn't recognize the topping—it looked like squashed marshmallows, but Aunt Collette said it was tofu. Tofu, really? You'd think it would be illegal to put something so healthy, so rubbery on top of a pizza. At least the spongy squares were easy to pick off. Soon we were flopping on the couch, chowing slices, watching reality TV and debating what movie to watch On Demand (Mem decided on *School of Rock*). It was after midnight before we called it quits. I slept in my clothes on top of the made bed that night, looking forward to sleeping in.

Fat chance. The Crayola crayon clock on the wall said 7:50 when Aunt Collette flew in the next morning. "Rise 'n' shine, darling," she sang. "Sorry I have to wake you, but I'm due at the store. Remember's been up for a couple hours already."

"Doing what?" I yawned.

"Watching The Weather Channel. It's his favorite, that and *Jeopardy*. Listen, I gotta go, but don't worry, I don't always have to work this early. See you around three." She hit the stairs before I even sat up.

Sure enough, Mem was sitting cross-legged on the living room floor watching Martin the Meteorologist explain the weather map. He didn't even glance my way when I walked in.

"You eat yet?" I asked, my voice scratchy from getting up too early.

"You eat yet?" he said, then whispered, "Eat yet?"

"Well, do you want something?" I asked.

No answer.

"I'll take that for a yes."

No one's ever going to accuse Aunt Collette of keeping a well-stocked kitchen, that's for sure—unless you crave things like plain yogurt, soy milk and flaxseed cereal, that is. I was about to give up when I happened to open the vegetable crisper and struck gold: a carton of Twinkies and a six-pack of strawberry milk. I gathered up the booty and brought it into the living room, where I set it between Mem and me on the floor. Mem broke off the tip of a Twinkie and sucked the cream filling out, then threw the spongy shell back in the box and took out another one.

"Mem, that's disgusting."

"I only like the middles," he said with a mouthful of white stuff.

"Yeah, but can you put your rejects somewhere else?"

He looked at me wide-eyed, like he'd never thought of that, then hurried to deliver the shells to the kitchen. "Done," he called, wiping a cloud of crumbs into the air as he returned. "Done done dee done."

"Good. Hey, let's watch something else." I reached for the remote.

"No!" he yelled. And I mean yelled. His face turned red and mad, and he snatched the remote before I could touch it. "I'm watching this."

"Fine—chill, will you?" Talk about touchy. I wondered what would happen if I rearranged his bedroom furniture or something.

At least I had Niko's Pizza Palace to look forward to. A couple of my friends were meeting there for lunch. If I stretched out my shower, read some magazines cover to cover, and maybe played with the ferrets, I figured I could survive the morning while Weather Boy mind-melded with Martin the Meteorologist. I guzzled the last slug of pink milk and headed upstairs to dig out my toothbrush.

When the crayon clock finally said noon, I put Linguini back in her cage with Jambalaya and headed downstairs. Mem was still doing the lotus position in front of the tube.

"Let's go," I told him.

No response.

"C'mon, let's get going."

Finally he turned my way. "We're going somewhere?"

"Yeah, Niko's, lunch."

I was afraid he'd throw another fit about having to leave his beloved show, but he actually smiled and turned off the set himself. "Let's go. Let's get going," he beamed and started toward the door.

"Wait, Mem, you've got Twinkie guts on your face—here." I handed him a tissue, and he scrubbed his face like he was trying to sand it off.

"Now?" he said.

"Now." But I wasn't at all sure how this was going to work. There were way too many things that could go wrong.

The first thing went wrong before we even made it to the curb. Dirk Dempster, the kid who lives across the street from Mem, happens to be a total jerk. In fourth grade, he blamed me for the class fishbowl he shattered, and he's made trouble for me ever since—copying off my tests and then accusing me of being the cheater, making sure I get picked last on teams, cutting ahead in line, you name it. He's the tallest, meanest kid I know. I think the reason he gets out of bed in the morning is to outdo his nastiness from the day before. I always steer clear of him, but now he was shooting hoops in his driveway. When he spotted us he shouted, "Hey, it's The Dipp."

I was going to ignore him, but then he started singing, "Dippity do da, dippity ay, my oh my, what a wonderful day." To make things worse, Mem thought it was funny and started waving at the idiot and saying what a cool guy he was.

Obviously, I had to say something, and what came out of my mouth was, "Shut up, Dirk." Dirk kept singing though, so I added extra loudly, "Come on, Mem, we'll take care of him later."

"Okay, we'll take care of him later," Mem said cheerfully and way too loudly. "We'll take care of him. Later."

"Yeah, right," Dirk scoffed and went back to shooting hoops.

Yeah, right? That was all? No—no way. Knowing Dirk, it wasn't going to be over that easy. But I didn't have time to worry about it because the second thing went wrong a minute later. We weren't halfway down the street when Mem scrunched up his face and came to a dead standstill in the middle of the road.

"What's the matter?" I said.

"My shoes hurt."

"You got a stone in them or something?"

"A stone or something? No, they just hurt."

I eyed his sneakers, the same sneakers he was wearing yesterday and all morning today. "You gotta get rid of them then."

"No!" he bellowed so fiercely you'd think I was trying to turn off The Weather Channel.

"Fine, we'll keep them. But let's go back and get you another pair for now."

"Don't have another pair," he pouted, and then he just stood there, right in the middle of the road. Even when a car backed out of a driveway and headed toward him, he played statue, and I had to motion the car around him.

"All right, Mem," I sighed once the collision was averted. "Here, you wear my flip flops." I walked barefoot the rest of the way, carrying his sneakers and wishing I could throttle him on the spot. He was the reason I had to get up so early, the reason I'd gotten into it with Dirk, the reason I was going to be late to meet my friends, the reason my whole summer was going to be a bust. And what was he doing? Humming "Zippity Doo-Da," that's what.

When we finally reached Niko's Pizza Palace, my best friends, Reed and Mo (for Montgomery), were lounging at our regular table by the window. And— what was this?—Mo's twin sister Jo (for Josephine) was with them. The guys were negotiating pizza toppings, and Jo was inspecting a pile of coins in her hand.

"Mem, you know Mo and Reed," I said, pulling up two chairs. "And this is Jo."

"She's pretty," Mem said, his eyeballs popping out as if to touch her. It was the first time I ever saw him look someone in the eye for longer than a flash.

On cue, Mo started snickering and motioning

SHIRLEY REVA VERNICK

Mem to take the seat next to Jo, sticking me at the far end of the table. Then Mo started whistling "Here Comes the Bride."

"Knock it off, Mo," Jo said. "I've seen Mem around. Nice to finally meet you."

"Yup," he said, staring at his lap. "Really, really nice. To meet you."

"You're not at Hull Central. Do you go to private school or something?"

"Yup."

"Do you board?"

"I'm never bored."

"No, I mean..." She glanced at me and back at Mem, who was still staring at her all gaga. Then she started studying her pocket change again.

"Whatcha doing with all that money?" Mem asked.

"Looking for American Samoa," she answered, turning a coin over.

"American who?" he asked, and if he hadn't, I would have.

"American Samoa," she said. "I'm collecting all the state quarters. I have almost all of them, but not American Samoa."

"Not American some more," Mem said. "American some more."

"Hey, let's order already," she said, standing up and shoving the coins in her pocket. "Half cheese, half pepperoni, right?"

"Can I come?" Mem asked, prompting more laughs from Mo and Reed.

"Uh, I'm only going to the counter, but sure."

When the two of them were out of earshot, Mo leaned toward me and said, "How's it feel, having your cousin move in on your crush?"

"Yeah, right." I couldn't think of any other comeback, so that's how I answered, but I hated that it was the same comeback Dirk the Jerk had used on me just a few minutes ago. Truth is, I couldn't deny liking Jo. Her family is part Abenaki Native American, and she's got these big black eyes and long black hair and a killer smile. Mo does too, but it doesn't look half as good on him.

"I don't know what you see in her anyway," Mo said.

"That's because she's your sister," I answered.

"No, it's because she's the queen of mean."

"Not true."

"Dude, I live with her. Believe me, she's a snob."

"Well, I think— " I glanced up at Jo and lost my train of thought. She was looking at me from the counter. Smiling slightly. Curling her hair around

SHIRLEY REVA VERNICK

one finger. When our eyes connected, she burst into a full smile, just for a second, then turned to Mem.

"What's the deal, anyway?" Reed asked. "With Mem, I mean."

"Huh?— Oh, my mom's away on business, so I have to stay with my Aunt Collette and watch Mem while she works."

Reed peeked over his shoulder at Mem, who was still staring down Jo at the counter. "How long?"

"All summer."

"Ouch."

"Yeah," I muttered. And then Jo and Mem were back, Mem with a can of Dr. Pepper and Jo with a bunch of paper plates and napkins.

"You guys got quiet all of a sudden," Jo smirked. "What are we interrupting?"

"Nothing," I said quickly. "Hey Reed, how about some foosball?"

"Sure," he said, cracking his knuckles. We ended up playing until the pizza arrived.

"Is hot," Niko said in his Italian accent as he set the pizza on the table. Niko is one of those guys who looks like he belongs on the football field or in the boxing ring—bulging biceps, massive hands, face etched with little scars. Lucky for us and everyone else, he's as mellow as they come. He sliced the pie and was about to leave when he noticed Mem's sneakers sitting on an empty chair behind us. "Who is barefoot?" he asked.

It took me a minute to realize it was me. "Oh, Niko, sorry." I quickly forced my toes into Mem's small shoes.

"Don't do it again," he barked grumpily and walked away.

Wow, where was the laid-back Niko I knew, and who was this imposter? "What's up with him?" I asked.

"Maybe he's hungry," Mem suggested, helping himself to a slice.

"Yeah, maybe he's hungry," Jo pretended to agree.

"Whatever," said Mo. "So, we going swimming later?"

"I'm in," said Reed with a mouthful. "What about you, Johnny?"

"I—I'm free at three...uh, are you going, Jo?"

"Can't—I'm due at Patsy's in a few minutes."

Before I could say anything else, Reed leaned into my ear and whispered, "Guess you'll have to wait to find out how she looks in her bikini."

"I heard that," Jo glared at Reed. "You know what—I'm outta here. See you, Mem." She stood up, put a slice of pizza on her napkin, and mouthed, "Sorry, Johnny," before heading out the door.

"See you," Mem said as the door jangled behind her.

"Nice going, Reed," I said, but he only laughed and grabbed another slice.

"Nice going is right, Reed," Mo chimed in. "She left without chipping in her share. Now we each gotta pay an extra buck."

That's when I realized I was stuck paying for both Mem and me. "Hey Mem, you got any money?" I asked on the off chance he might have a couple dollars.

"Yup, here." He pulled a $50 bill out of his pocket. Fifty dollars.

"Jeez, where'd you get that—Aunt Collette?"

"Nope."

"Where then?"

He produced a pack of Juicy Fruit gum. "Same place as this."

"Where?" I asked for the third time.

"Where? My friend. My friend Chip."

"That a kid at your school?"

"Your school? Nope."

It didn't really matter where it came from—cash is cash. Mo snatched the bill out of Mem's

hand and said, "We'll get you change, buddy...
unless you wanna buy us another pizza first,
that is."

"No way," I snapped. "Don't anybody ask Mem
for money, except me. Got it?"

Mo shrugged, "Only kidding." He scrambled
to the counter and paid Niko, then we all hit the
sidewalk together.

"See you later," I told Reed and Mo, who were
heading in the opposite direction. "Call me for— "
and then to make sure Mem wouldn't invite himself
along, I stood behind him and mimed swimming.
Mem turned around in time to catch the last bit
of my aerial backstroke, but he didn't get it—at
least, I don't think he did. At any rate, he didn't say
anything, and that was a relief.

It was a long walk home without any shoes,
without any friends, without anything to fill the rest
of my shift with Mem. Luckily, Mem closeted himself
in his room when we got back, so I set up my
GameCube and played a few rounds of StarBender.
My mom called at one point just to check in; I did
the good-doobie thing and told her, "Everything's
fine. We're having a pretty all right time."

"Really, Johnny?" she said.

"Yeah, sure."

"Good. Because I can tell I'm going to love this project, but I can only do it if I know you're happy."

"Happy as a clam, Mom." Not.

"I'll call again in a couple of days then. Hi to Collette."

"Got it."

"And don't forget to floss."

"Goodbye, Mom."

Aunt Collette got home a little late, her ruby lipstick gone and her eyes striped with those little veins that pop out when you're tired. Mem gave her a celebrity's welcome and begged her to play Trouble, which he'd already set up in his room. As for me, I hotfooted it to the lake to meet Mo and Reed, and I didn't feel guilty at all for not taking Mem with me.

Well, hardly at all.

Chapter 3

The next day I got to stay in bed a little later since Aunt Collette didn't have to be at work until eleven. Mem had been watching The Weather Channel all morning, but when I came downstairs he leaped up and was all over me. "Let's go swimming, Johnny! C'mon, let's go swimming at the lake."

"What—do you even know how?" I asked groggily.

"Do you even know how?" And then I realized he was already wearing his trunks.

Okay, I thought, *this might not be the worst way to spend the day.* I guess I was still half asleep, or I wouldn't have had such a crazy thought. "You sure you can swim?"

"Yup. I learned at school."

"They have a pool at your school?"

"Yup." He took a pair of swim goggles out of his shirt pocket and pulled them over his head. "But I wanna swim in the lake."

So it was settled. I stumbled into my trunks and stuffed some towels and Twinkies into my backpack before I was even fully awake. My flip flops were nowhere to be found, though—until I looked at Mem's feet. "You really don't have any other shoes?" I asked.

"Nope. Do you?"

I threw on my sneakers, which still felt like homework and smelled like the cafeteria, and told Mem to get a move on. All I wanted was to hit the beach and get barefoot again. Then maybe I could relax for a while.

No such luck. As we started down the front steps, something caught my eye. The mailbox. It was different somehow. I squinted against the morning glare. Something was definitely off, but what? I ran down the driveway. Now I saw. The letters didn't say T E DIPP anymore. They said DOPE. Someone had removed the T, put the E where the second P had been, and gone to all the trouble of buying an O to replace the I.

Dirk the Jerk. I was sure of it. I could just see him, that mop-topped, freckle-frosted freak, prowling around Aunt Collette's yard when no one was looking. DOPE. Did he really think that being captain of the basketball team entitled him to pull a stunt like this? "C'mon, Mem," I charged into the street. "We're taking a little detour."

"Why?"

"We need to go to the hardware store."

"Why?"

I scoped Dirk's mailbox and the gold-and-black lettering that read A. DEMPSTER. "I don't know, but I'll figure it out."

Mem's face was getting red and twisted, so I knew an outburst was on its way. Sure enough, he planted his skinny little body in front of me and screeched, "But we're going swimming at the lake! Johnny, I wanna go swimming. At the lake. I know how. I learned at school. We have a pool there. You prrrrromisssssed!"

Great, a temper tantrum right out here for the world to see. Maybe even for Dirk the Jerk to see. Mem was acting two and I felt 99. "Okay Mem, fine, you're right," I said. "I told you we could go to the lake, and we will. It's just that we can stay there longer if I get this errand out of the way first. You want to stay at the lake as long as possible, don't you?"

"Don't you?" he said, his voice softer now. "Don't you?" He started walking with me—not very fast, but at least in the right direction. "Don't you?"

Champlain Hardware is right next door to Niko's. I hadn't been there in ages, but when Mem and I stepped inside, it smelled familiar, like the paints and varnishes my dad used to keep in the garage, back in the good old days. Mr. Wizzly, the owner, greeted us from behind the counter. I asked him where he kept the letter decals.

"Next to the *No Trespassing* and *For Sale By Owner* signs," he said, pointing to the back of the store.

Good, I could work in private there. So while Mem picked out the letters of his name, I racked my brains. Dempster, Dempster, what could I do with Dempster? It needed to be something really maddening—no, infuriating—but what? Then finally I had it. I took a U and a B—black on gold—and made Mem put his stack of letters away while I paid. I asked Mr. Wizzly for my three dollars change in quarters.

"Ub?" said Mem on the way out. "Or is it bu?"

"Neither." I put the decals in my backpack. "I'll tell you later. Maybe."

"Okay. Want some Juicy Fruit?"

"No. Hey, let's say hi to your mom while we're here." The 7-11 was right around the corner, and I figured it would fill up some of the blank time that was stretching out in front of us like a school day.

"Yeah!" he shouted and started off faster than I'd seen him go in two days. He got there first. By the time I arrived, Aunt Collette was already pouring him a slushie the color of her lipstick.

"Howdy, Johnny," she said over the moan of the slushie machine. "Good timing, you two—I was about to die of loneliness." She handed Mem his drink and started pouring my favorite, blue raspberry. "What're you boys up to?"

"We're going to the lake," Mem slurped. "We're going swimming because I know how. But first we had to— "

"Hey Mem, you know what?" I cut him off. "I'll take a piece of that Juicy Fruit, after all."

He handed me a stick of stale gum and, thankfully, that was enough to make him switch gears. "Good day for the beach today, folks," he channeled Martin the Meteorologist in all his squeaky enthusiasm. "Clear and sunny this afternoon, partly cloudy and cooler tonight. This is Martin the Meteorologist wishing you blue skies and starry nights."

"Sounds good," Aunt Collette said, picking a *People* magazine off the rack and perching on her stool with it. "Now, what did you say brought you downtown?"

Just then, the door sleigh bells jangled, and Niko walked in, although he looked more like a gangster than the perky pizza guy I'd always known. He was wearing the same grimace he had on when he caught me barefoot yesterday. His apron was stained blood-red with tomato sauce, and his sunglasses, roosting on his forehead, were like an extra set of beady eyes. "Two packs Gold Strikes," he rasped when he got to the counter.

Aunt Collette raised her eyebrows into triangles of surprise. "And hello to you too, Niko."

He made a weak laugh and smoothed his mustache. "I am sorry. It's just that I—I need my smokes."

"I thought you quit."

"Today I am not quit. Maybe tomorrow." He laid down his money.

She frowned but got him his cigarettes anyway. "You okay, Niko?"

"I am...tired."

"Now *that* I can appreciate." She winked at Mem. "I wouldn't mind a good night's sleep myself one of these days."

"Sleep is good. Better than these." He rattled the Gold Strikes boxes. "Well, I..." He kept his mouth open, but no words came out, and he finally turned to go. "See you."

Aunt Collette watched him leave and then wondered aloud as she closed the cash register, "Now, what do you suppose has gotten into him?"

"That's what I want to know," I said. But before we could toss any guesses around, Mem was at the door begging to go to the beach. "C'mon, Johnny. You promised. Let's go swimming at the lake! I know how! You promised!"

"All right, all right," I said, draining my slushie cup. "Let's go."

"We'll have supper when I get home," Aunt Collette called after us. "Around seven."

Only a few other kids were swimming when we got to the lake—no one I particularly knew—and a man and a small boy were sitting on a wooden raft about fifty feet out, fishing. The bass and pike really bite this time of year, and I could see the boy yanking something on the end of his pole. His father—or whoever the man was—leaned over and helped him with the reel, but the fish got away.

I wondered what my own father was doing

right now. Not thinking about me, that's for sure. Even when he lived with Mom and me, he spent all his free time hiding in his basement workshop. It never would have crossed his mind to spend a morning at the lake with me. I wondered if that kid on the raft knew how lucky he was, even if the stinking fish did get away.

Mem and I picked a spot on the sandy-stony beach and spread out our towels. *Okay*, I supposed as I took off my shirt and lay down, *this should be tolerable. Dull and friendless, but tolerable.* Mem kicked off his—I mean my—flip flops and ran straight into the water, which was still freezing cold at the end of June. He lasted about three minutes, then bolted back to his towel and gobbled a couple of Twinkies guts before going shell-hunting. I dug my *Sports Illustrated* out of my backpack and escaped into an article about yacht racing. I had to admit, this was kind of all right. Mem was entertaining himself, and I could chill. Yes, this was working out okay.

Okay, that is, until Mem disappeared a half-hour later. One minute I could hear him crunching around on the sand, and the next minute he was gone. I sat up to inspect the thin strip of beach—nothing. I stood up to scan the lake—nothing. I ran knee-deep into the water and called his name over and over, louder and louder—nothing. The other kids were gawking at me, and I think the man on the raft was too.

I didn't know what to do. What if he were drowning right this very minute? What if he already had drowned? It would be all my fault. Visions of police cars and lake-rakers raided my mind, and my heart started pummeling my chest. I turned back toward the beach.

And there he was, wrapping himself in his towel and digging around for more Twinkies. "Jeez, Mem," I hollered. "Where were you?"

He finished decapitating his Twinkie before he answered. "Picking shells. I told you I was."

"Didn't you hear me calling?"

"Nope. You mad?"

"Yes—I mean, no—I mean..." I didn't know what I meant. "Where're your shells anyway?"

He pointed somewhere behind him. "In my special place."

"Well, your special place almost gave me a heart attack." I put my shirt back on and packed up my towel. "Let's go." My throat was so tense, the words came out in spurts.

"You are mad," he moaned and started drawing a picture in the sand with his toes. "You are too, aren't you?"

"Look, from now on, try to stay where I can see you, all right?"

"Where I can see you. All right. Where I can see you. See you."

Mem must have been tired or bored because he didn't put up a fuss about leaving. We didn't talk during the walk back, and then I marched straight into the shower. I must've taken a pound of the beach home with me, plus I was hot, so the water felt good. When my blood pressure finally returned to normal, I got out and went to my room for some peace. But instead of finding privacy, I found Mem on my bed playing with the ferrets.

I coughed loudly to make him notice me. He glanced up. Whatever he saw on my face made him jump to his feet, rush Linguini back into the cage, and slip off to his own room with Jambalaya, all without a word. I think he was scared of me. He probably thought I was still angry, but I wasn't. I wasn't angry, I was just...I don't know...glad I wasn't him.

It seemed like forever until Aunt Collette got home and another eternity until she and Mem went to bed. Sometime after midnight they finally turned in, freeing me to take care of my business with Dirk.

The decals had gotten a little wet from the towels in my backpack, but not too bad. I snuck a flashlight out of the kitchen and peeked out the living room window to make sure the Dempster's house was dark. Everything was a go, so I opened the front door, closed it gently behind me, and sneaked down the front steps in my bare feet.

Slinking along the grass, I realized I was smiling. It's not that I loved the idea of messing with someone else's stuff, but still, I felt like Tom Sawyer or something, doing mischief for a good cause. If only I had Mo or Reed along as my Huck Finn, this might be downright fun.

When I got to the Dempster's mailbox, I turned on the flashlight long enough to peel off the first E and the P, changing A. DEMPSTER into A. D_M_STER. Then I took my time applying the U and the B I'd bought from Mr. Wizzly. I wanted the letters to be neat and straight, as if they had always spelled A. DUMBSTER. That way, it would take Dirk some time to get it. He'd have to look at the mailbox for an extra second and wonder if it were really any different at all. Then he'd stand there, humiliated, trying to figure out exactly which letters had changed. I only hoped I'd get to see his face when all that happened.

Perfect, I thought, stepping back to admire my handiwork. This was perfect. With those two little letters I was getting Dirk back for all the names he ever called me and all the pranks he ever framed me for. I should've thought of this ages ago. Before going back inside, I ripped the D off Aunt Collette's mailbox. I'd forgotten to get new letters for DIPPY, but OPE was better than DOPE. Now nothing stood between me and a good night's sleep.

Nothing except Mem, who appeared without warning on the porch. "Hi, Johnny," he called in his too-loud voice, tying his bathrobe around his scrawny waist. "Whatcha do— "

"Shhhhh! Mem, what're you doing here?"

"Watching you," he whispered cheerfully.

I opened the front door and motioned him inside. "Look, Mem, out there, I was just..."

"Mailing a letter?"

"Yeah, right, I was mailing a letter." Two letters, to be exact.

"Why don't you talk to him instead? He lives right across the street."

Talk to Dirk the Jerk? That'd be the day. But I told Mem I'd think about it for next time. "Why are you up, anyway?" I asked.

"Up, anyway? I heard Jambalaya crying, so

I went to be with her. You weren't there, so I came downstairs to look for you. Up, anyway?"

Great, now he was monitoring my every move. Didn't he ever hear of personal space? "Hey, how'd you know it was Jambalaya crying and not Linguini?" I asked.

"Easy. Linguini never cries, only Jambalaya."

"Yeah, but Mem..." I began, then stopped myself. I didn't really want to get into a late-night debate with him over ferrets or anything else. I wanted to relish my mailbox master stroke, maybe gloat a little to myself, alone. So I told Mem I'd keep an ear out for the ferrets, and we both headed upstairs. I was going to sleep like a log.

SHIRLEY REVA VERNICK

Chapter 4

Early—too early—the next morning, Aunt Collette and
Mem dropped me off at my house to mow the lawn.
Mr. Boots' old dog Millie was roaming around out front,
and she started barking her muzzle off when we pulled
into the driveway. She hates everyone except cranky
old Mr. Boots, so she yowls at anyone who walks by.

As soon as I got out of the car, Millie stiffened,
bared her teeth, and growled viciously. I'm used
to it, but I was sure Mem would freak. Then the
strangest thing happened. Mem got out of the car,
and Millie started wagging herself in circles. When
Mem held out his hand, she bounced straight over to
him and let him pet her—let him actually touch her.
I couldn't believe my eyes.

"Wow, Mem, this never happens," I remarked.

"Well, it's not like Mem's a stranger here," said Aunt Collette.

"Neither am I," I said, "but you don't see Millie doing her happy dance on me." No, Mem had a special touch with animals, especially the crying ferret and yapping mutt varieties.

After giving Millie a final squeeze, Mem got back in the car. Aunt Collette said she'd pick me up after her hair appointment. "In about an hour," she said. "That enough time?"

"Yeah, sure." Millie whined softly as the car backed out of the driveway, then she turned around and started barking at me all over again. "Go on, get," I scolded as I climbed the porch steps. "I've got work to do."

Mr. Boots took his time answering the door. Finally, he appeared at the screen, pulling on his bathrobe and reading glasses. "Yes?" he grunted through his grey-white stubble of beard.

"I came to mow the lawn."

He couldn't hear me over the dog's racket. "What's that you say?"

"I'm here to mow the lawn. The lawn."

He opened the door long enough to let Millie in. "I'll open the garage," he said, and before I could say thanks, he let the door slam. That figures. Mr. Boots is about as social as a prune pit. He's probably what kids like Dirk Dempster turn into when they grow old.

As I pushed the mower on laps across the yard, I started wondering if Dirk the Jerk had gone out to shoot hoops yet this morning. I didn't want to miss the look on his face when he noticed his mailbox. Hopefully he was still in bed, like any normal person would be at this hour; it wasn't even eight o'clock yet.

When I finished the lawn, I put the mower back in the garage and waited for Aunt Collette under our willow tree, thinking how good a glass of my mom's black-cherry iced tea would taste about now. Sweat was swimming down my face, and my stomach was growling louder than Millie—which was too bad for me because Aunt Collette was late.

It's a good thing I recognized my aunt's car when she finally showed up, because I'd never have recognized my aunt. In the space of one morning she'd gone from long brown hair to short blond locks with a streak of purple in the front. She was a cross between Tinkerbell and Cruella de Vil—a real hack job.

"What do you think?" she asked as I piled in.
"It's…"
"Quite a change, huh?"
"That's for sure."

"My friend Holly—she does my hair—well, her niece was there, and she talked me into it. Cost me another parking ticket too," she laughed, pointing to the fresh violation notice that joined the old ones under her windshield wiper. Aunt Collette always lets a stack of tickets collect there, announcing her bad parking karma to the world, until she gets around to paying them. "You like my new 'do, don't you, Remember?"

"Nope." It must be nice to be able to say whatever you want and not have people get mad at you.

"Well, you know what they say about hair," she said.

"You've gotta comb it every day?" Mem guessed.

"It'll always grow back," she said, eying herself in the rear-view mirror as she drove. "And I sure hope it's true. Now, I'm gonna drop you boys off and run. I'm working late tonight—that darn punk again. But don't you worry—I've got tomorrow off."

"Yay, tomorrow off!" Mem shouted. "Tomorrow off off!" I wanted to jump for joy too, but I kept quiet.

"Everybody out," Aunt Collette announced, grinding her wheels against the curb as she pulled up to the house. "You're on your own for supper, but if you want to stop by the store later, there might be a snack in it for you."

Mem headed straight inside for The Weather Channel. I planted myself on the porch with my Gameboy and a bag of whole wheat pretzels. There was no sign of Dirk yet, not even a telltale basketball in the driveway, so I figured I could still catch the show. He'd probably be coming out any minute now, and I'd have my moment of glory.

But he didn't show, not after half an hour, not after a full hour. Maybe it was still too early, or maybe he was out of town. Of course, there was also the possibility that he'd already seen his mailbox and was busy plotting some terrible revenge. I decided to think this over from the safety of the living room.

"It's gonna be a hot one," Mem said, pointing to Martin the Meteorologist.

"I know."

"Wanna go swimming?"

"Maybe later. Hold on, I need to use the phone." I went to the kitchen and called Reed's house but only got his voicemail. Mo wasn't home either, but Jo answered, so at least I got to talk to her. She said Mo was at the lumberyard with their father picking out wood for their new deck. Jo had her friend Patsy over, and they were on their way to Hair by Holly to get their nails painted.

"You just missed my aunt there," I told her.

"Got a hatchet job. Her hair's short as mine now, plus two shades of weird."

"Really?" Jo sounded fascinated. "Maybe we'll stop by the 7-11 on our way. Well, see ya."

"See ya." I hung up and ran into the living room. "C'mon, Mem, let's go visit your mom." I couldn't wait around for Dirk the Jerk any longer, not when there might be a chance to "bump into" Jo.

We were halfway through our 7-11 slushies when Jo and Patsy arrived. Jo looked like she'd walked off the cover of a tennis magazine, with her white skirt, white polo t-shirt and gold skin sizzling in the shafts of sunlight that poured through the windows. This was definitely worth missing Dirk's face at the mailbox. I opened my mouth to say hi, but Jo and Patsy flew past me and ran straight to the counter.

"Ms. Dippy? Is that you?" Jo gasped.

"In the flesh. You like?"

"It's outrageous—I love it!"

Patsy said she agreed, and the three of them started rattling on about hair color and how a little change is good for everyone. It was like I wasn't even there. Not a wave, not a hello, nothing. I might as well have been one of the floor tiles they were standing on.

After a while Mem said, "Hi, Jo!" and she finally tossed us a glance.

"Hey Mem," she smiled. "How are ya, buddy?"

"How are ya, buddy? Good! How are ya, buddy?"

"Remember, you know these girls?" Aunt Collette asked.

"Nope," he said. "Just Jo."

"Well, this is Patsy," Jo said. "Now you know both of us. So, you guys hanging out?"

"Mem wanted to visit his mom," I said, and it was true, sort of. He did want to visit her once I suggested it.

"Cool," she said. "Well, gotta split. See you around?"

"Yeah, I have tomorrow off, so...yeah." I wanted to say more, but words abandoned me.

"Wishing you blue skies and starry nights," Mem said, which they apparently thought was adorable. They gave him big waves and cooed, "Same to you," and said good-bye to him about ten more times before they finally bounced out of the store.

"Nice girls," commented Aunt Collette.

"Yup, real nice," Mem agreed, which made Aunt Collette crack up. Then all of a sudden she started acting like she was in a hurry to get back to work.

Remember Dippy   45

"Uh, Johnny," she said, talking fast, "I see Remember has taken over your flip flops. Here, here's a five spot. Why don't you two go over to the drugstore and see if you can find yourself a new pair?" She set the money on the counter and started putting on her lipstick, even though she already had a coat of it on. "Go on now, both of you. Shoo."

She obviously wanted to get rid of us, so I pocketed the money and turned toward the door, which is where I saw The Man for the first time. He was thumbing through the magazines near the cold drink case, sporting a cowboy hat and a flowery Bermuda shirt. He looked around my dad's age but in better shape, and I think he was trying to grow a mustache. For a minute I thought he might be my old gym teacher, but no, for the life of me, I couldn't place him.

The Man strolled up to the counter, and Aunt Collette instantly burst into a massive smile. I couldn't hear what they were saying, but Aunt Collette looked pretty happy to see him—happy and a little nervous. I started to step closer, but Mem, who didn't seem to notice The Man at all, was pulling on my arm and begging to go. I stole one last glance at Aunt Collette and gave up.

Mem kept running ahead of me on the sidewalk. "Why're you so excited about helping me pick out a lousy pair of flip flops?" I asked.

"Cuz. Cuz when you get the new ones, these old ones are definitely mine. Forever." Talk about simple wants.

When we were opposite Hair By Holly, I said, "Let's cross the street now." Mr. Literal instantly darted into the road without looking. I had to yank him back before he got pancaked by a minivan. "Mem, when I say let's cross now, I mean let's stop, check for traffic, and go when it's clear. Get it?"

"Get it?" he said blankly.

"Never mind. Just be careful, will you?"

As we passed Hair by Holly, I could see Jo through the window, sitting at a small table opposite Holly. I wanted to stay and watch, but I'd have died if they spotted me, so I ran to catch up with Mem. Three dollars and twenty-one cents later, I was wearing a pair of lime green flip flops and carrying my sneakers. This time, Patsy was at the manicure table when we walked by, and across the street The Man was unlocking his pick-up truck. I slowed down, trying to get a look at this guy's license plate—New Jersey—and the sign painted on his truck—Cappellucci Property and something. He took off down the street before I could read the rest.

"Hey Johnny," Mem said as we drifted along, "let's go back to the hardware store."

"What for?"

"What for?" He scanned the sidewalk like he was afraid someone would overhear. "I want to buy something," he whispered.

"Mem, you don't need any— " But wait, what else did we have to do all day? "Okay, fine, but you have to use your own money."

"Yup." He took off around the corner, and by the time I got to the store, he was busy poring over the letter decals.

"What're you doing?" I asked.

"I need letters. The small ones are okay, and they're only a quarter. I can get a lot." With that, he started collecting a stack of them.

Was he going to wallpaper Dirk's mailbox? "No, don't," I said. "This is a bad idea, Mem."

He stopped what he was doing. "You don't even know what my idea is," he said, looking off over my shoulder. His cheeks got red and his eyebrows squashed together, and I could tell he was breathing fast—the surefire signs that a hissy fit was brewing. Then Mem did something pretty

48   SHIRLEY REVA VERNICK

unexpected: he talked himself down. "Use your words," he muttered to himself, his fists clenched. "Mrs. Potts says use your words instead of your lungs. Try, don't cry. Talk, don't walk. Breathe, don't seethe. Flow, don't throw." Then he lifted his chin and said to me, "You can't tell me what to do with my own money, Johnny."

Impressive. He actually held it together. No screeching or stomping off or any of his other usual tricks. Plus, I had to admit it, he was right: I couldn't tell him how to spend his own money. Besides, there was no sense pressing my luck with his temper.

"Okay, Mem, fine," I said. "You do what you're doing, and I'll stand over here and look at the paint chips." I decided to amuse myself by counting how many shades of white there were. I was at 68 when Mem brought a mound of decals to the counter. I joined him just in time to hear Mr. Wizzly remark, "Seems to be a run on these things this week."

"What do you mean?" I asked, but what I really wanted to know was whether Dirk Dempster had been buying them.

"Selling like hotcakes," Mr. Wizzly answered. "Isn't that what you were here for the other day? You and some other folks. A regular hot item. That'll be five dollars and thirty-five cents...thank you, young man. He handed Mem his change, which didn't include any state quarters. Have fun."

"Have fun," Mem said.

"Always do," Mr. Wizzly winked.

Mem winked back.

When we got home, Mem stashed the decals in his room before parking himself and Jambalaya in front of the TV. *Okay, no immediate decal danger,* I decided. *Maybe he'll forget all about them.* Still, he was in an especially good mood—he even let me change the channel—so I wasn't done being suspicious. He was a man with a plan, and I had the feeling I was going to be the one to pay for it. Thankfully, he didn't carry out his scheme that day. He seemed happy to hang out in front of the tube, and all I had to do was make sure the Twinkies didn't run out.

One other weird thing did happen though toward evening, and I mean it was totally bizarre. I'd been in my room listening to tunes and lounging with Linguini, and then I went downstairs to call Mo. But I never made it to the phone. I was too amazed by the scene in the living room: Mem was playing my GameCube, and he'd gotten StarBender all the way to level 10! No one I know has ever gotten that video game beyond level 8, and I've never made it past 7.

"Mem? What—how—"

He jumped at the sound of my voice. "I was being careful with it, honest, Johnny," he pleaded.

"It's all right," I said. "But how do you know how to play?"

He shrugged. "My friend Chip. And school." Now that he sensed I wasn't going to holler at him, he turned his attention back to the game.

"You have video games at school?"

"Yup. This one's my favorite." With that, he advanced to level 11. "I like Olympiad too."

I sat down next to him on the floor. "Sounds like a pretty cool school."

"It's all right. I like summer better."

"Yeah, me too. You want to try a two-player round?"

"Yup," he said, handing me the other controller.

Mem won three straight games before I top-scored him once. Then we switched to Air Angler, and he got my guy every time.

"You should open your second parachute when I get that close," he said at one point.

"These guys have extra parachutes?" I asked.

"Yup. And the plane'll drop you a ladder if you go under the escape hatch."

Whoa. This was awesome. Not just the game,

but being able to play it with Mem—I mean, really play it. In my whole life, Mem and I had never played a legitimate, regulation game together. Mom always made me play cards and checkers with him, and then she made me let him win. Aunt Collette would try to let me off the hook, but Mom would insist, or she'd pressure me into playing stupid games like hide-and-seek or Marco Polo with him. Mem never "got" hide-and-seek because he was never willing to come out of his hiding place, even when he got caught. And he wouldn't keep his eyes closed for Marco Polo, so I always had to be It. Talk about lame. And boring.

But this—this was a real competition. I was free to try my hardest, and I wasn't guaranteed to win, not by a long shot. It was kind of like having Mo or Reed here. Well, maybe that's an exaggeration, but it was definitely better than being by myself, and that was a first. We played until Aunt Collette got home.

Chapter 5

I had the next day free because Aunt Collette was off from work. A whole day to myself—no taking care of Mem, no cutting the grass, nothing but taking it easy. The first thing I did was sleep until I felt like getting up—I didn't even hear Mem sneak in to get the ferrets—and then I wandered down to the kitchen to call Mo and Reed.

Aunt Collette was scooping coffee beans into the grinder and humming some country western song. She was wearing a striped beach dress and looking tired again, or maybe she just didn't have her lipstick on yet. "Morning, sunshine," she said. "Your mom called earlier. Want some joe? It's decaf."

"I'll give it a try."

"The way I like it—black—or the way Remember likes it—with enough cream and sugar to rot out all your teeth?"

"How about somewhere in between?"

"You got it." She turned on the grinder and took three mugs out of the dishwasher. They were the mugs Mom gave her last Christmas, with snowmen in Hawaiian shirts and sunglasses. The shirts reminded me of the one The Man was wearing yesterday, and I considered asking her about him, but then the phone rang.

"Hello?" Aunt Collette said, turning off the grinder. "Sure thing. Johnny?"

It was Mo. He wanted me to meet him and Reed at Niko's. Then maybe we'd take a spin on the bike path over in Chesterton. I told Mo to count me in and to order extra cheese if he got to Niko's first. I wanted plenty of sustenance for my first real day of summer vacation.

"Smells good," Mem said, taking a big theatrical whiff of air as he walked into the kitchen. Linguini toddled on one of his shoulders, and Jambalaya held on for dear life on the other.

"Coffee's almost ready," Aunt Collette told him. "Hey, I thought we'd drive up to Sugar Loaf today, see if they got the water slides turned on yet."

"Yeah!" he shouted. "Shoe Garloaf!"

"Sugar Loaf," Aunt Collette corrected him. "How about you, Johnny? Want to join us?"

"How about you, Johnny?" Mem chirped. "Shoe Garloaf. How about you?"

Every summer they turn Sugar Loaf ski slope into this outrageous water park. It's a blast—they even have go-carts you can take down the trails. I love that place, but I'd already made plans with my friends, so I couldn't go...could I? No. I hadn't gone biking with the guys in ages, and I was really looking forward to a whole day without Mr. Tag-Along. Still, the water slides were epic, and besides, Mem wasn't totally terrible company. Then again, what would Mo and Reed think?

"Thanks, Aunt Collette," I finally answered, "but I'm busy."

"All right," she said, pouring our drinks. "Long as you have something to do. I brought some turkey roll-ups home last night. You can help yourself."

"Okay," I said, but what I was really in the mood for were those steak and pepper subs they sell at Sugar Loaf.

No sign of Dirk when I headed out to meet the guys. His mailbox still said A. DUMBSTER, and ours still said OPE. The suspense was starting to get to me, I'll admit. Well, at least Mem would be out of the house most of the day, away from those pesky decals he was hiding somewhere. I was going to have to keep a careful eye on him.

Mo's and Reed's bikes were already parked in front of Niko's when I got there, so I hopped off mine and strolled in. They were hanging out at our usual table—taking up two seats each—and watching some golf tournament on the little black-and-white counter TV. That part of the scene was normal. But in the opposite corner lurked unexpected catastrophe: Jo and Patsy were standing by the jukebox with none other than Dirk the Jerk, and they were all talking to each other! Granted, it was mostly Patsy and Dirk talking, but Jo was definitely part of it, laughing and waving her freshly painted nails around when she spoke.

So Dirk wasn't out of town. He must have seen his mailbox. And now he was chitchatting with Jo. I didn't like this one bit. Dirk Dempster was nothing but trouble, and now that he was buddying up to Jo, I hated him even more. I turned my face away from him, but I'm pretty sure he noticed me, even if the girls didn't. Once I made it to the table with Mo and Reed, I tried to ignore what was going

SHIRLEY REVA VERNICK

on by the jukebox, but I couldn't. The more I told myself to tune them out, the closer I listened. Patsy was saying that her brother just got his driver's license and was going to drive himself to a jazz concert in Burlington next week.

"Can't wait to get my license," Dirk said. "Wheels are freedom. I need some of that."

"Freedom from what?" Patsy asked.

"From home."

Jo and Patsy murmured something in agreement, and then Dirk started feeding money into the jukebox. "Here," he said. "I'll play you my theme song." In a minute, an old rock 'n' roll tune came on where this guy with a funny voice sings, "We gotta get out of this place, if it's the last thing we ever do. We gotta get out of this place. Girl, there's a better life for me and you."

I knew if I looked up, I'd see Patsy blushing— and Jo too probably. He was flirting with both of them.

"Hey Johnny," Mo said, tearing me away from my spying, "how about we try Demolition Hill after this?"

"You kidding?" I asked. "It's more like Suicide Hill unless you have a dirt bike, and last time I checked, none of us does." There's only so much rock and rut you can put regular wheels through without a trip to the emergency room—which, by the way, is four towns over. It was bad enough spending the summer working; I didn't want to spend it in a cast too.

"C'mon," Reed baited. "You aren't scared, are you?"

"Not scared. Smart." I pulled the menu out from between the salt-and-pepper shakers, pretending to read it. I felt my eyes being pulled to the jukebox though, and it took all my strength to keep them on the menu. *Stay focused*, I kept telling myself. *Stay focused*. I studied the list of pizza toppings: olives, eggplant, peppers, onions, mushrooms, bacon, pesto, pepperoni, BBQ chicken, artichokes. I read the appetizer list: garden salad, mozzarella sticks, antipasto, black bean dip. I was just about to start on the beverage list, but Jo was suddenly standing at our table. Now, that was more like it.

"Did you see Niko?" she asked.

I couldn't tell whether she was talking to all of us or just me, but Mo and Reed kept right on yakking about bikes, so I said, "No, I just got here. Why?"

"He looks awful," she whispered, taking the chair next to mine. "Check him out—there, over by the oven. See what I mean?"

Jo was right. Niko probably hadn't shaved in a week, and from the way his hair was sticking out from under his baseball cap, I bet he hadn't picked up a comb lately either. "You think he's sick?" I asked.

"You're not allowed to work around food if you're sick—with something catchy, anyway. I think he's got drama." She said the last word long and slow, like she was savoring the taste of it.

Then, as if he sensed us talking about him, Niko called out to us, "Hey, no feet on chairs. I tell you a hundred times."

"He's never told us that once," Mo complained, putting his feet on the floor. "What's his problem anyway?"

"Exactly," Jo said. She looked beautiful. Too bad Mo and Reed had to be here, but at least Mem wasn't around to hog her attention.

"Maybe he does have drama," I said. "He's even smoking cigarettes again. I saw him buy a couple of packs at my aunt's store."

"I wonder what it is," Jo said. "I wonder what we should do. Should we do something?"

"Well, I wouldn't try asking him about it, that's for sure," I said. "Not now, anyway. He's liable to bite your head off if you get too close."

"I guess." Suddenly Patsy was at her side, and they nodded to each other. Great, just when Jo and I were having an actual conversation. Just when I was able to make complete sentences that made some kind of sense. What were the chances of that happening again any time soon? Slim at best. "Okay, Johnny," Jo said. "Gotta run. See ya."

"See ya. Hey, we might be going to the lake later, so maybe…"

"Cool," she smiled.

Wow, I thought, *really? She really thinks it's a cool idea?*

"But I can't. C'mon Patsy." And she was gone.

As if getting turned down—in front of my friends—wasn't humiliating enough, Dirk the Jerk overheard it all, and he boomed, "Maybe it's your breath, Johnny boy." Even Mo and Reed laughed at that. My face felt as red as Niko's pizza sauce. If only I could turn back the clock and opt for Sugar Loaf, I could be skimming the water slides now instead of drowning in embarrassment.

"Forget Jo," Mo said when he finally stopped snickering. "What does she know, anyway?"

"More than you do," I answered. I didn't even get a chance to tell her I liked her nails.

"Let's just order," Reed offered. "C'mon,

Johnny, you've got all summer to work your way into Jo's schedule. And look—Dirk's leaving too."

The rest of the day went a lot better once Dirk was out of my hair. For one thing, the pizza was primo—crispy crust, loads of pepperoni, perfectly gooey cheese. Whatever was wrong with Niko, he was still in good enough shape to turn out a great pie. I'd have to let Jo know that. For another thing, we had an awesome bike ride. Reed actually did try Demolition Hill and made it to the bottom with nothing worse than a scraped knee. And to top it all off, Mo's mom made us a batch of her famous hotdog lasagna and invited Reed and me to spend the night.

Jo was sleeping over at Patsy's—rats—but the guys and I had a good time hanging out. I clobbered them in Scene It and stood my ground in Treasure Seekers, and then Mo brought out his golf clubs and indoor putting green. He cleared off the playroom floor, rolled out the fake grass, and plugged in the automatic ball return only to realize he couldn't find any balls.

"Well, that's the end of that," Reed griped.

"Not so fast," said Mo. "Hold on." He disappeared into the kitchen and returned with a handful of eggs.

"Mo, you've got to be kidding," I laughed.

"No worries," he said. "They're hard-boiled.

Mom's making egg salad tomorrow. She'll never miss a few."

So that's how we invented a new sport called Egg Whack. Mo actually wanted to call it Egg Roll, but Reed and I vetoed it on the grounds that it sounded like Chinese take-out. Anyway, if you think golf balls are hard to shoot into little holes, you should try it with eggs. They wobble all over the place and then abruptly stop. Their shells crack open, and the room starts to smell like sulfur. They're slow and unpredictable. It's a blast.

"Hey, you think it's true about a golf course coming to town?" Mo asked.

"No way," I said.

"The ground's all wrong for it," Reed agreed, "plus the season's way too short up here."

"Too bad," grumbled Mo, pushing his egg into the cup. Mo loves golf, but the only time he gets to play on a real course is during the first week of August, when he visits his grandparents in South Carolina. It's hard to get any good if you only play one week out of the year.

When our eggs refused to roll another inch, we DustBusted the fake grass and opened a window to get rid of the stink. "Well, boys," said Mo in a voice exactly like his mother's, "I see it's past midnight.

Shouldn't you be off to bed?" Reed and I cracked up, and then we decided to play video games.

After endless rounds of Guitar Hero, Night Drive, and Game On—most of which I lost—we put on Air Angler. "Prepare to get creamed, boys," I told them.

"No way," said Mo. "I've been practicing."

"Really? What level are you at?" I asked.

"Nine. Two levels higher than you."

"Sheesh," complained Reed, "I'm stuck at six."

"Well," I said, "you're both about to be blown out of the water."

We all manned our controls robotically for a while—we've played this game so much, we could probably do it with our backs to the screen. Then I pulled out my first secret weapon: the extra parachute.

"What the heck was that?" Mo asked as I captured his glider.

"Just what it looked like—a second chute."

"I never knew— "

"Now watch this," I said, dropping the escape ladder to dodge Reed's attack.

"Wait a minute," Reed said. "Is this a new version or something? My version doesn't have this stuff."

Remember Dippy   63

"Yup, it does," I said. I captured Mo's avatar and wasted Reed's satellite, ending the game with a stellar victory. "You just didn't know it. Neither did I, until Mem showed me."

"Mem?" they both said.

"Yeah, he's like a wizard or something. You should've seen him trounce me in Olympiad. We played for hours last night. New round?"

"Might as well," Reed said. Then, shaking his head, he added, "Must be nice having someone to hang out with at home. My brother's too young to be any use."

I rolled my eyes. "We're talking video games, Reed. It's not like he's normal. It's not like we can talk to each other or anything. He's still Mem."

Reed just shrugged and pressed the restart button.

We hit the hay late. I fell asleep thinking how great it would be to have the kind of older cousin who could teach me how to talk to girls and deal with cranky old neighbor dogs. But that was about as realistic as a golf course coming to Hull. Not happening.

Chapter 6

The next morning I was asleep on Mo's bedroom rug when something started tickling my arm. I tried brushing the fly—or whatever it was—away and rolled over to go back to sleep, but then I realized someone was whispering at me. "Johnny, Johnny wake up." Apparently it wasn't a bug.

I opened my eyes and saw Jo holding the phone over my face. "It's for you," she said, looking like she was fighting off laughter. I must've had major bed head or maybe drool running down my chin, but she was out of the room before I had a chance to be too embarrassed.

"Hello?" I croaked in my scratchy morning voice.

"Johnny." It was Aunt Collette, and she sounded serious. "I told you I had to be at work at nine today."

I squinted up at Mo's alarm clock—9:20. "Oh man, I'm sorry, Aunt Collette," I said, jumping up from under the blanket. "I'll be right home. Give me five minutes."

"I'm already at the store, sweetie." This time she didn't sound so mad. "Mem's with me. So get yourself over here, but don't break your neck doing it. And don't do this again, deal?"

"Deal."

"Oh. And Johnny, swing by the house on your way and pick up my 7-11 sweatshirt, will you? The AC's on overdrive today."

"I'll be right over."

Mo and Reed were still sound asleep—Mo was even snoring a little—so I threw my blanket on the bed and headed downstairs. Jo was pouring herself a bowl of some healthy-looking cereal when I walked through the kitchen. "Thanks," I said, handing her back the phone.

"What did you guys do yesterday?" she asked.

It was awesome that she wanted to know. And I wanted to tell her, but then I remembered what Dirk the Jerk had said about my breath, and I knew I hadn't brushed my teeth since the hotdog lasagna last night, so I took a few steps back and said, "Nothing. You?"

"Patsy's mom had to take her car into the dealer in Burlington, so we tagged along and she dropped us off at the movies. They were showing the original *Star Wars*."

"For real?"

"Yeah, it was great—worth having to listen to Patsy talk about Dirk Dempster the whole way there and back."

As usual, I didn't know what to say next, and besides, I had to scram. "Well, I gotta fly. So, uh, see ya."

"Okay," she said, reaching for the milk. "See ya."

Not exactly a romantic exit. I grabbed my bike from the garage and rode home wishing I'd asked Jo more about the movie or something, but I can never get the right words out around her—heck, I can barely get any words out around her. She must think I'm shy or uninterested or boring. I'd have to show her I wasn't any of those things...if I could only untie my tongue.

I didn't get to wallow in my misery over Jo for long. From about halfway down our street, I noticed more decals on our mailbox. I couldn't make the words out yet, but it definitely didn't say OPE anymore, and the mailbox door was ajar too. I biked faster.

TRY SCOPE. That's what the decals spelled, and inside the mailbox stood a bottle of Scope mouthwash. Dirk had even drawn a smiley face sticking out its tongue inside the O of SCOPE.

I didn't know how I was going to retaliate, but I was going to get that rat good. It was bad enough when he was making fun of Mem, but now it was personal. As soon as I could think something up, I'd even the score. In the meantime, I tossed the Scope bottle into the kitchen trash, found Aunt Collette's sweatshirt, and made tracks to the 7-11, hating Dirk Dempster more with each turn of my bike wheel.

Mem was paging through a paper by the news rack when I got there, and Aunt Collette had a line of customers at the cash register. I watched her talk and laugh. She has a knack for chatting with everybody about everything, or maybe about nothing. I wished I could do that around Jo.

"Hey," I said to Mem.

"Hey," he said without looking my way. For a second I thought he was mad at me for being late, but then I remembered that was his way.

"Whatcha looking for, the weather page?" I asked.

"Nope, just looking."

"Oh. So, how was Sugar Loaf? Did you ride the Flume of Fear?"

"Yup."

"Did Aunt Collette?"

"Once, then she threw up."

"Ouch."

He folded the newspaper and put it back on the rack. "Mom says we're supposed to get haircuts today."

"What? I don't need a haircut. And who's gonna pay for it?"

Mem batted the air as if to wave off my question. "Don't have to pay. Mom's friend Holly across the street, she always does mine for free. Guess she's gonna do you too. C'mon."

In the old days, you'd never catch Mem agreeing to get his hair cut. He used to get hysterical if anyone but Aunt Collette touched him, and even with her it was dicey when it came to his hair. He couldn't stand the feel of the tags in the back of his shirts either, and he always whined about his shoes feeling too tight no matter how loose they were. To this day he won't wear gloves. Or shirts without buttons. Or anything yellow or made of wool. To tell the truth, I don't know how he ever gets dressed in the morning.

"Come on, Johnny," he nagged.

"Fine." I glanced out the door toward Hair by Holly, but my eyes caught a different sight—The Man walking into the store. He was wearing the same cowboy hat and a different flowered shirt, but most of all, he was wearing a big fat grin the minute he spotted my aunt. He pretended to be rummaging for something in the freezer section until the line of customers dispersed, then bee-lined over to her and started gabbing.

Luckily, Aunt Collette hadn't noticed me yet. I wanted to know who this guy was and why he was hanging around so I handed Mem another newspaper and craned my ears in the direction of the counter. One thing I found out right away was how quiet The Man's voice was. I had to piece the conversation together from what Aunt Collette was saying.

"Hi there, TJ," she said. "How's things?... Oh, I had the day off yesterday. I hope my helper took good care of you...Ninety in the shade...Those? Those are my latest parking tickets. I collect them... Well, good luck with that. How long'll you be away?... Next Thursday? Well, I don't know. I'd sure love to, but I have my son and—gee, that's supposed to be the best restaurant going...I'll tell you what. You let me think it over and I'll let you know when you get back...Fly safe now, you hear?"

Aunt Collette was grinning to herself as The Man left. I didn't understand why she hadn't said yes to this date he was asking her on. Girls are so hard to figure out. All she had to do was say yes, and then he'd know she liked him, and since she already knew he liked her, they could relax and get on with it. Life would be a lot easier if people said what they meant, the way Mem does.

"That you over there, Johnny?" Aunt Collette called. "You come out from behind those papers and stop spying on me."

Oops. I wandered over and sat on the counter next to the cash register. "Sorry for being late."

"That's all right, sweetie, no worries," she said.

I watched her replace the spool of paper in the register, then I came out with it. "He likes you," I said.

"You think?"

"C'mon, Aunt Collette, give me the dirt."

"What dirt?"

"Fill me in on this guy. Is he your boyfriend?"

She laughed at that. "No."

"Do you want him to be your boyfriend?"

"Aren't you the little busybody? For your information, he's—oh, I don't know. It isn't that simple when you're my age."

"It isn't that simple when you're my age, either."

"You got girl troubles?"

"It's just that— " I didn't know whether to go on. Maybe Aunt Collette had some good advice. After all, she's a girl; she might understand Jo. But maybe she was just another adult who wouldn't get it.

"It's just what?"

"Nothing," I said, though part of me wished I hadn't. "So, you gonna go out with him?"

She looked over at Mem in the corner and exhaled noisily.

"You worried about who's gonna watch Mem?" I asked.

"Partly. You offering?"

"Yeah."

"Even after you've watched him all day?"

"Sure."

"Thanks, that's sweet of you. I'll let you know... Good morning there, girls."

I turned around to see Jo and Patsy standing behind me. Jo was holding two bottles of pink lemonade. Patsy had a bag of licorice in one hand and a box of chocolate-covered raisins in the other.

"Hi, Ms. Dippy," Patsy said.

"Morning," smiled Jo. "Hi, Johnny."

"H-hi." I could feel Aunt Collette watching me. I could feel her figuring out that Jo was The Girl.

"Looks like you're stocking up on all the good stuff," Aunt Collette said.

"We're going to the Majestic later," explained Jo.

"*Ferris Bueller's Day Off* is playing at one." Turning to me, she said, "You two want to join us?"

My cheeks started to burn. "Sounds good," I managed to say.

"Meet us out front."

"Great. So I'll, um, yeah. We'll just...right, so..."

Aunt Collette saved me from my stammering. "Now you and Mem skedaddle, you hear? Holly's probably twiddling her thumbs waiting for you."

"Right," I said. "See you later."

Jo set the lemonade bottles on the counter. "Make it ten till one."

Wow, I thought as I walked over to where Mem was still looking at the newspapers. *I think Jo just asked me out on a date!* "C'mon Mem," I said, "time to face the blade."

Mem was lost in the newspaper. "Hmm? Blade, what blade? Hey, it's Jo! Hi, Jo! Hi, Patsy! We're gonna get a haircut." As I dragged him by the arm, he called out, "Bye, Jo! Bye, Patsy! We're gonna face the blade. We're gonna get a haircut too."

Did I mention that I've never been inside a hair salon before? Buster's Barber Shop is where I go, and I like it there. You always know what you're going to get with Buster, plus he's fast. Walking into Hair by Holly with its light-up mirrors and sit-under hair-dryers and shelves of styling goop felt like crashing into Oz.

"Can I help you?" said a girl who didn't look much older than Mem. She was standing behind the counter. If this was Oz, then she was the wicked witch's daughter—dyed-black hair, thick black eyeliner, and black lipstick that accented her permanent scowl. From what I could see of her, she was what my mother would call well-upholstered and what Dirk the Jerk would probably call porky—round face, plump arms, and dimples where her knuckles belonged.

"We're here for Holly," I said.

The girl flipped her hair behind her ear, revealing about ten metal studs. "Holly went home sick. But I can help you if you want. I'm Leesha." She closed the magazine she'd been reading and hopped off her stool, letting her gauzy black dress graze the floor. She must have been six feet tall. I wanted to grab Mem and run back to Kansas. One look at Mem and I knew he was feeling the same way.

"Y'know," I said, "we're not in any rush. Maybe we'll come back another day."

"Suit yourself," she scoffed, a dozen silver bracelets clinking at her wrists. "But Aunt Holly will take a lot more hair off than I will."

Now she had my attention.

"No matter what you tell her, she always gives guys crop-tops, especially in the summer."

"Holly was going to do it for free," I said.

Leesha's eyes narrowed, and she stared at me hawk-like for what felt like a long time. "Whatever," she finally mumbled, walking over to the first haircutting station and motioning us to follow her. I nodded to Mem, and he came along with me, but he was rubbing his hands together so I knew he was nervous.

Wow, what a set-up. There was a phone, a potted plant, a mini-TV, framed photos, a coffee pot, a clock, and a tiny boom box, all there in the space between the chair and the mirror. The only thing Buster the barber has on his shelf is a set of combs and scissors soaking in that blue cleaning liquid.

"Who's first?" Leesha asked, patting the swivel chair.

"Who's first?" Mem said to the floor. "Who's first?"

Leesha looked confused. "You tell me."

"You go, Johnny," he said.

"That's okay, Mem. You go."

"No. You go first."

"But I had the first turn the other day with... um...Trouble. Yeah, and with the shower. You should have the first turn today."

Mem started inching backwards. I thought I'd have to give in and be the guinea pig, but Leesha saved me. "You've got better hair," she told him. "I'd rather work on yours anyway." Then she tossed a sneer my way.

Mem studied his hair in the mirror. He glanced at Leesha, then at the door, then at me. I thought this might be Mem's way of telling me he wanted to bolt—which was fine by me—but instead of darting out, he shuffled over to the swivel chair and took a seat. "I'm gonna have the first turn," he told her. "Cuz Johnny got the first shower yesterday, that's why."

"If you say so," she said.

"Yeah, I say so."

Mem sat quietly enough while she put a plastic cloak over him—nice and loose, like I told her. He even tolerated it when she combed his hair and fluffed it with her fingers. But when she revealed her shears, he got squirmy. She kept trying to snip, and he kept jerking away and turning around to make sure I was still there.

"Hey, you're gonna get hurt," Leesha scolded him, "and I'm not gonna get in trouble just because you can't sit still, so cut it out."

Now Mem was rocking back and forth in the chair, white-knuckling the armrests. "Cut it out?" he asked suspiciously. "But you're the one who's supposed to be cutting it. No, Holly is. Holly's supposed to cut it. I want Holly. Holly! Holllllllyyyyy!" And just like that, he was off the deep end, gonzo.

Leesha jumped back in a six-foot flurry of black gauze. "What is wrong with you?" she cried, looking back and forth between her scissors and the crazy kid in her chair, like she was trying to figure out if her shears had actually driven him insane. She'd obviously never met anyone like Mem.

I was about to call the whole thing quits, when I had a brainstorm. "You get cable by any chance?" I shouted over Mem's wailing.

"Don't know," she shouted back. "Why?"

"Try channel 47, The Weather Channel."

Skirting Mem, she went over to the mini-TV and clicked it on. Hooray for all of us, there was a mini-Marty the Meteorologist happily predicting rain. Mem eased back into the chair, wide-eyed and serene, as if Marty had hypnotized him through the tube.

"Good, now do his hair," I said. "Quick, before they cut to a commercial."

"You guys are weird," she muttered. That's the first time anybody ever lumped me into the same category as Mem. Oh well, who cared what this freaky girl thought?

"He's got great ends," Leesha told me as she worked. "Nice and light. He'd be perfect for a little color."

"Color?" I cringed.

"Yeah, like maybe gold. Or bronze. What do you think?"

"I think you're nuts."

"Just offering." She didn't say another word until she was done with Mem's head. Then she unsnapped his cloak and asked him if he liked it.

Mem stood up and examined his reflection for a long time. "No. But I like how my hair looks."

"Wait, what?" asked Leesha.

I translated, "I think what he means is, he didn't like getting his hair cut, but he likes the results. Right, Mem?"

"Right, Mem? Your turn, Johnny."

I had to admit, Mem's hair looked pretty good—normal, just a shorter version of what he already had. Still, the idea of letting the wicked-witch-in-training go after me with a sharp instrument didn't exactly thrill me, and I hesitated.

"Your turn, Johnny," Leesha mimicked, folding her pudgy arms like I was taking too much of her precious time.

"Fine," I said, taking a seat. "But aren't you a little young to be a hairdresser?"

"Not if you know how to manage the system."

"What system?"

"Look, do you want a trim or not?"

"Fine, but only take off a little. I like the back of my neck covered."

"Chill, will you?" She tightened the cloak around my neck like a tourniquet. "I told you I don't do crop-tops. I'm an artist."

I didn't need an artist. I needed a trim, and I didn't trust her, so I watched every hair she snipped, and she knew it.

"You can breathe now," she said at last. "I'm done with the scissors. Let's get this dried, and you're good to go. You want gel?"

"What does it do?" I asked.

"Just makes your hair hold its shape. No big."

I considered whether Jo might like me better with more shape. "Okay, but only a little."

Leesha mushed the gel, which smelled like cucumbers, into my hair and spun me around to face her and her blow-drying gun. A noisy blast of hot air hit me, and I had to close my eyes against the gale force. I'd never had my hair dried for me, and it felt kind of nice once I got used to the heat. After a while, she turned off the dryer and plumped my hair with her fingers.

"All right," she said. "You've got a good head there once you groove a little style into it. Take a peek."

She turned me around. When I glimpsed myself in the mirror, I couldn't speak. I couldn't move. I couldn't believe it. Who was this alien with the spikes and the poufs staring back at me? *Somebody, please tell me this is all smoke and mirrors, a big joke.* But it wasn't. I looked like a rock star on a bad hair day, only worse.

Fighting the impulse to scream, I managed a weak "wow," which Leesha thought was a compliment. She uncloaked me and repositioned a couple of the spikes. "Now, I took off the bare minimum in back," she fussed, "so I should see you again in four to six weeks."

In your dreams, Leesha. "Well, thanks," I murmured. "Right, Mem?"

Mem was glued to The Weather Channel again, and it took him a minute to pull himself away. When he did, he didn't seem to notice my hair crisis. "Well, thanks," he said. "Wishing you blue skies."

"Any time," Leesha purred. "And tell your friends."

I'd tell my friends, all right. I'd tell them to steer clear of this house of horrors—that is, if I could ever face them again. "C'mon, Mem." I poked my head out the door to make sure no one I knew was passing by. I'd die if I bumped into the guys or Jo. Thankfully, the street was bare for the moment so I stepped outside and motioned Mem to follow. "Let's go," I said and started running down the sidewalk toward Niko's.

"But your bike's across the street," Mem panted.

"Never mind, we'll get it later."

"I wish I knew how to ride a bike."

"I'll teach you sometime—just hurry."

Mercifully, Niko's was empty—too early yet for lunch—so I sat Mem at a table and told him to watch TV or read the menu or do whatever he wanted as long as he stayed in that chair. Then I raced past the counter and the kitchen into the bathroom. With the door locked behind me, I bent over the sink and ran the hot water full blast. The spikes on my head were as stiff as icicles, but they finally melted under the steamy water. Half a roll of paper towels later, my hair looked more or less like I'd just washed it. Hallelujah. I was going to go straight home and do a real washing, with extra shampoo and lots of elbow grease.

Except, that's not what happened.

On my way up front to retrieve Mem, I caught a glimpse of Niko that stopped me short. He was crouching on his hands and knees with his face pressed to the kitchen floor, talking to himself in Italian. "Niko, are you okay?" I called, thinking he was hurt or sick or gone crazy or something. He'd been looking so awful lately. Maybe he'd collapsed right there on the floor.

"Fine, just perfect," he grumbled, standing up, all hot in the face. He looked worse than ever, and an open pack of cigarettes was hanging out of his shirt pocket. "What you want, pepperoni this time?"

"No, actually I just stopped by to use the—are you sure you're all right?" I stepped into the kitchen. As I did, I realized he'd been bent over the heating vent. I looked at the floor and then over to Niko's pitiful face, and I knew something bad was going on.

"No, I am not all right," he snorted, leaning against the dishwasher and staring at the vent. "Not one little bit all right. My whole life is down that pipe." He took off his baseball cap and rubbed his bald spot. "Gone. Kaput."

"What are you talking about, Niko?"

"It is not your worry."

"Maybe I can help."

He emitted a small laugh to let me know how ridiculous he thought that was.

"Why don't you just tell me?" I said.

"Okay, fine. You want to know? I tell you." He massaged his sagging eyebrows. "It is my grandmother's ring. I was to give it to my Carmelita, ask her to marry me. Last week I stand here, right here, and hold it up to the light. I clean it, make it ready for Carmelita. But I drop it, and it runs across floor." He made two fingers run through the air. "When I chase after ring, I kick it by accident, and it slips down that pipe. Damn pipe."

I stood over the vent. "Have you tried— ?"

"I try everything. Day and night I try. And I try to get help. But everyone tells me how old and—what is the word?—delicate these pipes are, and tangled up too. Would cost thousands and thousands to dig up and replace—more than ring is worth. I have not slept since Thursday last."

Wow, this was bad. Niko's love life was literally down the drain. "What did the ring look like?" I asked.

"Beautiful, gorgeous. Round diamond in middle with rubies on sides. Platinum, not gold. Platinum is better than gold, stronger. My grandfather knew jewelry."

"You should propose anyway," I said.

"No." He stared at me with burning eyes. "Not without ring. I will not."

Remember Dippy   83

Just then, a man's voice came from the counter, "Hello? You open?"

Niko shrugged and put his cap back on. "First customer of day. I need every customer I can get if I am to buy another ring for Carmelita."

Poor Niko. No wonder he was grouchy these days. Well, at least this gave me something to talk to Jo about. She was dying to know what was up with him, and I might be the only person in town who knew.

I found Mem twirling the plastic foosball players and had to coax him away by challenging him to a race back to the house. As soon as we got home, I ran straight into the shower to rinse off those loose hairs you get after a haircut. I took an extra long soak to try to wash away my rotten morning. Rotten oversleeping, rotten mailbox, rotten haircut, rotten luck for Niko. What else could possibly go wrong? I wondered sourly. And what did I do to deserve all this?

The hot water ran out after twenty minutes, so I grudgingly got out of the shower. When I went to my room for a change of clothes, a pleasant surprise lifted my spirits a little: Mem had used his letter decals to spell LINGUINI and JAMBALAYA on the ferrets' cage—not to deface anyone's mailbox. Was I ever relieved.

SHIRLEY REVA VERNICK

I held the furry guys and gave them each a bit of a chocolate kiss, then stretched out on the bed with them—I hadn't gotten nearly enough sleep last night. The next thing I knew, I was dreaming about swimming in the lake, only the lake was filled with hair gel, and when I stepped out, my hair looked like a peacock's tail so I covered my head with seaweed until I got home. Weird. That girl Leesha really did a number on me.

When I woke up, the ferrets were walking around on the floor, and the crayon clock said almost two. Two o'clock. The movie with Jo! My first date with her, and I slept right through it. How stupid could I be? I bolted downstairs to phone her house—not that she'd be there, but at least I could leave a message. As I cut through the living room, I expected to see Mem parked in front of the TV, but he wasn't. Oh well, I'd look for him after my call. Fortunately, Mo was home, and he picked up.

"Mo, sorry for running out this morning—I had to work."

"No prob. What's up?"

"Listen, would you give Jo a message? Would you tell her I'm sorry. Like, really, really sorry."

"Why, what'd you do?"

"Nothing, I just forgot—no, don't say that.

Remember Dippy   85

Don't say I forgot. Tell her, I don't know, tell her something came up."

"Whatever."

"Look, I gotta go find Mem."

"Later."

"Yeah." I really hoped he'd say the right thing to Jo.

Mem, it turned out, was sitting on the front steps drinking a Dr. Pepper. "Whatcha been up to?" I asked, perching myself on the railing.

"Nothing. My friend Chip stopped by. We played Olympiad."

"Is he any good?"

"Yup, but I'm better."

"Did he give you any money this time?"

Mem shaded his eyes with one hand and peered up at me. "That was for my birthday. Usually he just brings gum."

"Oh."

"He gave me gumballs this time, a whole box. Want some?"

"No, no thanks."

"Hey Johnny, do you think the branch up there on that tree would hold me?" He pointed to a slender, leafy limb that grew parallel to the ground and made a puddle of shade on the yard.

"Don't know," I said. "Looks a little skinny. Why?"

"Why?" He gazed at the branch admiringly. "Why? Nothing, it just looks like a special place."

"Yeah, well, let's not try out any new special places, not when you're with me, okay?"

"Wanna play Apples to Apples?" he asked. I didn't know whether that meant he'd heard me or not. But there wasn't anything else to do, so we played.

I tried calling Jo again after supper, but her mom said she couldn't come to the phone right now. She didn't call me back either.

Chapter 7

The next day it turned July, and that whole week
passed in a blur. Aunt Collette was working extra
hours because she had to fire the kid she called
the punk, which meant she had to fill in the hours
herself. Mo and Jo went away with their parents
for the Independence Day holiday, and Reed had
to help his grandmother move in with his family. I
mowed Aunt Collette's yard and my yard (with old
Mr. Boots glaring at me from his front porch), and
my dad called to say hi on his way to his cruise, but
mostly it was Mem and me knocking around the
house. We hit the lake once, and I tried to teach him
how to ride my bike a couple of times, but that was
a flop. Dirk the Jerk didn't seem to be around so
we didn't have him hassling us. I didn't do anything

about the mailboxes, mostly because I didn't have any good ideas.

Then finally it was the weekend, and although I was still doing double shifts with Mem, at least my friends were back. Of course they were back— no one misses the Hull Berry Blast. Every year on the Sunday after the Fourth of July, the farmers' co-op throws a big strawberry shortcake festival at Imogene Park. If you can stand the mosquitoes, you don't want to miss it. One dollar buys you all the strawberry shortcake you can eat, and for a little extra, you can add hotdogs, fries, soda and ice cream. Almost everyone shows up.

Imogene Park was already packed when Mo, Reed, Mem and I arrived. Families had spread blankets on the grass and were feasting on the food they'd bought or brought. Kids and grown-ups were lined up at the shortcake table, waiting for the co-op people to dish them out a heaping dessert. And in the corner, Hull's own oldies band, Purple Rush, was playing "Heat Wave."

Mo and Reed dashed to the hotdog cart, but Mem and I had already demolished a box of toaster waffles at home, so we went straight to the shortcake line. Ahead of us were some other kids from school, our mailman and his family, my old baseball coach, and—

holy cow—Leesha, the giant Goth girl who'd massacred my hair. She was standing alone near the front of the line, still wearing twice her weight in jewelry, and this time she'd added a black headscarf and boots to her get-up. Fortunately, she didn't see me, or maybe she was ignoring me. I didn't care either way.

Mem, who was busy scanning the crowd on the lawn, didn't notice Leesha, but soon he started grinning from ear to ear, which could only mean one thing. Sure enough, Jo was just arriving, with Patsy. "Jo! Hi, Jo!" he hollered, waving both hands. "Jo, over here!"

"Cut it out, Mem," I hissed, pulling his arms down.

"Why?"

"Because you're embarrassing me."

"But I want Jo to come on over and have shortcut with us. Don't you? Don't you want her to have strawberry shortcut with us?"

"Yes. No. I mean, I don't know, but acting like a goof isn't going to get her over here."

"Yes, it is." He was grinning again, and when I turned around, Jo and Patsy were getting in line with us.

"Hi, guys," Jo said. Did this mean Jo didn't hate me for blowing off the movie?

"Hi! Hi, Jo! Hi, Patsy!" Mem glowed, although he was looking at the grass, not at them. "Told you, Johnny."

"Told him what?" asked Jo.

"Nothing," I said.

"I told him— "

"Nothing. Listen, about the movie last week..."

"I'm over it," she said, but she didn't look particularly over it.

"Okay, but let me tell you what happened. See, I...first of all...well..." Why couldn't I form sentences with her? "I screwed up. Sorry."

"It was boring anyway," Patsy said. "You're lucky you didn't have to sit through it."

Jo gave her a look, only I didn't know what it meant.

"I told you, Johnny, I told you!" Mem started in again.

I had to change the subject pronto. Fortunately, I remembered I had actual news to tell her. "Hey Jo, I found out why Niko's been looking so bad."

Jo's eyes widened, and she and Patsy stepped closer. Mem zeroed in on a brown mutt that had wandered over. He plunked himself on the ground to play with it.

"So yeah," I said, "I talked to him. Turns out

Remember Dippy   97

he lost something really important. The diamond ring he was going to give to his girlfriend."

"He lost it?" Jo asked.

"He has a girlfriend?" Patsy asked.

And then they were both talking at once. "Who is she?" they wanted to know. "How'd he lose it? Did he lose it, or was he robbed? How'd you get him to tell you?"

"Who?" Mem asked, tuning back in for the moment.

"Mem and I were there the other day," I said. "I found Niko on his hands and knees in the kitchen—the ring fell down a floor vent. It was his grandmother's. He wanted to give it to this Carmelita lady, but he doesn't think he can get it back."

"Why not? Why can't he just— " Patsy started, but then someone was calling her name. It was Dirk. He was standing by the dinner cart with a hotdog in one hand and a bottle of mustard in the other. "Hey Patsy!" he shouted again. He was wearing his basketball uniform, so he must have just come from a practice. Or maybe not. Maybe he just wanted to make sure everyone knew he was the captain of the ball team.

Patsy glanced up, but she was so engrossed in Niko's problems, she didn't give Dirk the hero's welcome he probably expected. Instead, she held up a wait-a-minute finger.

"Does Niko's grandmother know this happened—is she still alive?" Jo asked, and Patsy leaned in to hear the answer.

"Is she still alive?" Mem parroted, still stroking the dog. "Still alive, still alive?"

"Don't know." That's what I said, but what I was thinking was, *good—Dirk gets to see me with Jo and Patsy*. Patsy had raised her pointer finger to him, so there was nothing he could do but glare my way and give his mustard bottle a shake. This was awesome, and then it got even better...

The wrong end of Dirk's mustard bottle was pointing up, so when he shook the bottle, instead of smothering his hotdog in mustard, he drenched his face and hair with it. Yellow nose, yellow chin, yellow cowlicks, gooey yellow everything. He was seething. It was hilarious. Too bad the others didn't see it. Too bad I didn't have a camera.

Dirk used his shirt to wipe the mustard off himself, and when his face reappeared, it was ketchup red. Scowling and mouthing words I couldn't make out, he flung his hotdog on the grass and vanished. Instantly, the brown mutt Mem had been petting plowed over and devoured the meat and

Remember Dippy   93

the bun, leaving no sign that Dirk the Jerk had ever been there.

"So yeah, I don't know about the grandmother," I said, "but I do know he won't ask Carmelita to marry him until he can afford a new ring."

"That's dumb," said Patsy.

"That's romantic," said Jo.

Now we were at the front of the line. Jo and Patsy got their shortcake, and then Jo said, "Thanks for the scoop, guys. We're gonna go find Dirk now. Keep us posted though, okay?"

"But..." I said, then realized there was no point protesting. I had to be satisfied knowing Dirk had run away with egg—I mean, mustard—on his face.

"Wishing you blue skies and starry nights," Mem said, but they were already lost in the crowd.

Mem and I got our cake and caught up with Mo and Reed near the band. I noticed Leesha sitting with her Aunt Holly at the picnic table across the park, but I couldn't spot Jo anywhere. Oh well, it had been nice while it lasted.

The guys and I ate ourselves silly on shortcake—well, Mem only ate the whipped cream part, the same way he eats Twinkies. In between mouthfuls, he sang along with the band at the top of his lungs, even though he didn't know the lyrics,

SHIRLEY REVA VERNICK

even though he couldn't carry a tune. He thought the words to "Satisfaction" were "I can't get no chain reaction," and when the band played "America the Beautiful," he crooned, "Oh beautiful voracious pies, forever waves of pain." At first, I pretended I didn't know him, but that was pretty impossible since he was either right next to me or calling to me every other minute. So I decided to ignore the people who were looking at us funny and just have fun tossing around the Frisbee Mo had brought. It's a free country, after all—Mem could sing if he wanted to. And he did want to. Finally, when it got too buggy for comfort, we called it a night.

Sometimes my best ideas hit me when I'm not thinking about them, and that's what happened on the way home from Imogene Park. I'd been racking my brains for a week without any inspiration for Dirk the Jerk's mailbox, and then, right when I forgot about it, *Eureka*!

"Mem, you wait here," I said when we got to our driveway.

"Why?"

"Because."

"Because why?"

"Because...because I need you to count for

me. I need you to stand there and count, and see if I can do what I need to do before you get to a hundred. Can you do that? Please?"

"Can you do that please?" he said solemnly. "One, two, three— "

"Not that fast. Try one thousand one, one thousand two, like that."

"Okay. One thousand, two thousand, three thousand..."

"Good, Mem. Keep going." I didn't have any decals, but I didn't need any. I ran over to Dirk's mailbox, which still said A. DUMBSTER, and peeled off the B and the E so it said A. DUM_ST_R. Then I rearranged those letters to spell MUSTARD. Mustard! This was going to burn Dirk to a crisp. I was beaming when I got back to Mem. Revenge tasted sweeter than strawberry shortcake.

"Eighty-three thousand," he said.

"So I did it—cool."

"What was that, anyhow?" he asked as we walked up the driveway.

"Huh? Oh, I was just, you know, sending Dirk some more letters."

"No, you weren't." He stopped on the front step and stared at me under the porch light. "My friend Chip says somebody's up to no good."

"Tell your friend Chip to lighten up," I said, holding the door open for him. But Mem just stood there, and I began to worry that he was going to squeal on me to Aunt Collette. "It's supposed to be funny, that's all," I added. "Come on, let's play StarBender." Finally, he followed me.

As we walked inside, I heard Aunt Collette in the kitchen saying, "Oops, gotta go," and hanging up the phone. "Howdy, boys," she called to us. "Was the park rocking tonight?"

"Yup," Mem answered, and that was all he said. Mem may be a lot of things, but I guess he's not a snitch.

"Maybe I'll make it there next year," she said, joining us in the living room. "If I can get some decent help at the store by then. You guys gonna crash?"

"Yeah, I'm wiped," I said.

"But what about StarBender?" Mem asked.

"Oh, right. I'm gonna pound him at this game first."

Mem thought that was hysterical, and he started guffawing in big coughs. "I'll cream you, Johnny! I'll cream you, you wait!"

"Well, I'm zonked," Aunt Collette said. "There's cauliflower chowder in the 'fridge if you get hungry."

Remember Dippy   97

Hungry? I felt like it would be days before I could think about eating again, especially when the menu was cauliflower chowder. So Mem set up StarBender, and we played video games until we couldn't keep our eyes open. I lost by a landslide, but I still felt triumphant...in a mustardy, dastardly way. Dirk Dempster probably went to bed tonight thinking no one had seen him make a mess of himself at the park. That would all change in the morning. One look at his mailbox and he'd know just how wrong he'd been. Then he'd have to wonder who else I might have told, only he couldn't ask anyone because then he'd be spilling the beans himself. This was perfect.

When Mem and I finally dragged ourselves upstairs, I noticed that Aunt Collette's light was still on, which was pretty unusual at this hour, so I poked my head in. She was in her bathrobe, standing in front of her closet and thumbing through her clothes.

"Hi," I said from the doorway.

"Hey," she said, turning around. "C'mon in."

I sat down on her bed, which was covered with magazines and crossword puzzle books, like she was prepared for a night of insomnia.

"Everything okay?" she asked.

"Yeah, fine. You going somewhere?" I motioned toward the closet.

"Naw, just taking stock. Guess I wasn't as tired as I thought."

"Oh." Funny, when I can't sleep, it never crosses my mind to take inventory of my wardrobe. I'd rather listen to tunes or count sheep, things you can do lying down.

"How was the chowder—did you try it?" she asked.

"Couldn't. Too stuffed with shortcake."

"It's not my best batch. I ran out of soy milk in the middle of making it."

Cauliflower and soy milk? Just the thought of it was enough to give me nightmares.

"Don't worry," she said. "I'll make another pot of it before the summer's out."

"Great." I sat there for another minute while Aunt Collette kept up her hanger flipping, but there didn't seem to be anything else to say, so I stood up to leave. "See you in the morning, then."

"Wait." She turned around and motioned me to sit back down. "Since you're here, there is something I want to talk to you about." She joined me at the foot of the bed and bit her lip. "I've decided to take your advice." She cleared her throat and smoothed what was left of her hair. "You know, about TJ, about going out with him."

"Cool. Is that why you're going through your wardrobe?"

"Yup," she said, just like Mem. "Listen, I know this is short notice, but he wants to take me out to dinner tomorrow. So if it's not a problem— "

"No worries, Aunt Collette," I said, which earned me a hug so tight I thought I heard a rib crack.

"Johnny, I know you haven't had much of a summer, watching Remember all the time. You probably haven't had a good summer since"—and here her jaw tensed—"since your father decided that having a family cut into his free time too much. I mean, sorry. I'm sorry to vent. He just makes me so mad."

"Yeah," I mumbled. "He makes me mad too."

"You know, when you were born, I was so happy for you, that you'd have two parents to take care of you instead of just one, like Remember. And I was so happy for your mom too, that she'd have someone to help raise you. I just can't believe he walked out on the two of you." She looked like she might cry.

"It's okay, Aunt Collette," I said, but I didn't mean it. It was most definitely not okay that Dad discarded Mom and deserted me. Granted, we didn't see much of him even when he lived at home, but at least we knew he was there. At least we could tell ourselves he cared. Now the act was over. Dad had Princess Kim and his house in Maine and a long-distance kid. And what really makes me mad is, no matter how angry I am at him, I still miss him, and he doesn't deserve that.

"Well," Aunt Collette sniffed, "you deserve a regular kid summer. As soon as I hire a new clerk, you'll get more time with your friends, I promise."

A regular kid summer. That was something Mem would never ever get—because he wasn't a regular kid. He didn't seem to notice that, but Aunt Collette did, and it made me kind of sad. I thought about the video game tricks Mem taught me, and how he didn't snitch on my mailbox pranks, and how he was willing to get the first haircut. "You know," I said, "Mem comes right along with me and my friends."

"And that's...okay?"

"Pretty much. Well, it depends, but yeah, pretty much."

"He especially likes your girlfriend Jo," Aunt Collette said.

"She's not my girlfriend."

"Okay." She folded her arms and squinted her eyes. "But, to quote you, do you want her to be your girlfriend?"

"Why, you want to double date?"

"Very funny."

"Oh, and just for the record," I said, pointing to her closet, "I like that white dress with the blue."

"That's a nightgown," she said, and we both laughed.

Now, this was the point where I was supposed to say good night and leave the room, but there was something I'd been wanting to ask her, and this seemed like as good a time as any. "Aunt Collette, why do you leave your parking tickets on your car all the time? I mean, isn't it embarrassing?"

"Well..." she drawled, putting her arm around my shoulder, "I see it like this. I think people get caught for the worst acts they do in life. So if the most dreadful thing I do is park on the wrong side of the street, that's pretty darn good, don't you think? Those tickets are like good-behavior medals. It's all those people who don't get fined when their meter expires who should be embarrassed, because that means they're doing even rottener deeds. You see?"

"I'm not sure."

"Why don't you sleep on it," she said and hugged me again.

Chapter 8

The next day was not a good day to lose Mem.
We'd gone outside early to make sure nothing had
happened to our mailbox, then I gave Mem another
bike-riding lesson. We played Operation, made tuna
sandwiches for lunch, and the next thing I knew
he was gone, disappeared, nowhere. I searched the
house (including the entertainment center) and
hollered out the living room window, but he was
either out of range or ignoring me. I even turned on
The Weather Channel to bait him, but it didn't work.
This was one of those times that Mem was strictly a
job, and a tough one to boot.

When he was missing for a solid hour, I went
out on the front porch to call him and was thinking
I should probably get on my bike and cruise the

neighborhood. Dirk was out shooting hoops, and if he'd been anyone else, I'd have asked right away if he'd seen Mem. I wanted to ask him—I was getting worried—but it seemed awfully chancy. While I weighed the risks, I watched Dirk dribble and shoot for a minute, and that was my big mistake.

"What're you staring at, doofus?" he shouted.

Before I could say anything, Dirk slammed his basketball down and started tromping across the street toward me. He looked mad. And big. I didn't know what to do, but my feet decided to meet him in the yard and plant themselves right in front of him.

"I've had it with you," Dirk snarled.

"What do you mean?" I asked, figuring my only hope was to play dumb.

"You know exactly what I mean," he breathed down at me. "Now you're gonna pay." He pushed me hard, and it was all I could do to stay upright. "I'm gonna pound you."

This is it, I thought. *My body as I know it will soon be replaced by a pile of shredded flesh.* If only my feet had taken me inside instead of here on the open battlefield, I might have escaped pulverization. Now it was all over.

Then the most amazing thing happened. Things—I couldn't tell what they were, exactly—

started pelting Dirk, first on his butt, then on his punching arm. Stones seemed to be falling from the sky directly over him, and he winced in pain. We both looked up, but I'm the only one who saw Mem crouching on the tree branch, almost completely hidden by leaves, shooting gumballs down. He had perfect aim.

Dirk freaked. The "rocks" kept hitting him, faster and faster, harder and harder. He couldn't get a grip on what they were or where they were coming from. Swearing and rubbing his backside, he ran across the street and disappeared into his house. And here I was in one piece, with nothing injured except a little pride. In that moment, I loved my cousin for making trees into special places and having friends who brought gumballs. I gazed up at him and gave him a hand salute, but he had his nose in the gumball box so he didn't see me.

Mem didn't come down right away. When he finally showed up in my room, chewing a big wad of gum and trying to whistle at the same time, I was lying on my bed, listening to my iPod. "Hey, thanks," I said, sitting up and unplugging.

"Hmm?" he said as he extracted Jambalaya from her little hammock.

"Thanks for helping me get rid of Dirk."

"Oh." He sat on the floor and stroked the ferret for a minute. "Fighting's bad."

"I know."

"Talking's good. That's what we learned in school."

"Talk? To Dirk Dempster?" I scoffed.

"Talk? To Dirk Dempster?" he said.

"I can't talk to him, Mem."

"Mrs. Potts says do what's right—talk, don't fight. That's what Mrs. Potts tells us."

"Do kids fight a lot at your school?"

"Sometimes," he shrugged. "Sometimes kids get really mad all of a sudden and they start to fight with someone. Mrs. Potts says it's not on purpose."

"Do you ever fight with anyone there?"

He didn't answer.

"Does anyone ever fight with you?" I asked.

Without another word, he got up and rushed out of the room with Jambalaya; a minute later I heard The Weather Channel snap on. I wanted to tell Mem I could help him with that, but I wasn't sure I could. I mean, look how I'd handled Dirk. Mishandled him is more like it. I'd be a mangled mess right now if not for Mem's magic gumballs. As I put my earphones back in, I had to wonder who was taking care of who this summer.

SHIRLEY REVA VERNICK

‏⁓

Dirk was more than enough unwanted company for one day, but more came anyway. It was almost six o'clock—right around the time Aunt Collette was due home from the store—when the doorbell rang for the first time all summer. I was afraid it was going to be Dirk again, or worse, Dirk's parents, and my first impulse was to take cover under my bed. Then I got this crazy idea that it might be Jo, in which case I'd want to answer it right away.

"I'll get it," I told Mem, but he was so caught up with Marty the Meteorologist, I don't think he even heard the bell. When I got to the door, I opened it an inch, just enough to see that it wasn't a Dempster. It seemed to be a girl. Not Jo, but a girl. I opened the door the rest of the way.

"Leesha?" I said. What was the giant gel-happy scissors queen doing here?

"My Aunt Holly told me to meet her here," she said flatly. "We're gonna help Collette get ready for her date."

Leesha had her hair in a bunch of braids, some that were her regular inky black and others that were dyed the color of fire engines or fresh peas. She looked like a traffic light, except that traffic lights don't frown all the time. I hoped Aunt Collette wasn't really going to let Leesha loose on her hair tonight, but then again, if TJ liked her with that purple streak, I guess he'd like her no matter what.

"So, can I come in or what?" Leesha demanded. As if I had a choice. She stepped into the living room and said hi to Mem, who unglued himself from the TV barely long enough to wave.

"Hey, you have a ferret?" she gushed when she saw Jambalaya perched on Mem's shoulder.

"You have a ferret?" he said.

"No, but my brother used to," she said, not realizing he was just up to his parrot tricks.

"Oh. I got two of them."

By this time, Leesha was squatting on the floor next to Mem. "Can I hold him?"

"Her," he said, handing Jambalaya gently over.

"She's so sweet. What's her name?"

"Jambalaya."

"Hi, Jamby baby," she cooed. "My brother's ferret was a biter. Can I see your other one?"

"Yup." The two of them got up and went to my room. Weird, but it saved me from having to make conversation with anyone. I grabbed a bottle of water and waited with a magazine at the kitchen table for the two aunts to show up.

Aunt Collette got here first, looking a little flushed. "Where's Holly? Isn't she here yet? Oh no, Johnny, I was going to bring home something for your supper tonight but I forgot, I was in such a rush. Do you want me to go back out?"

"We're fine," I said. "There's still the cauliflower chowder from last night."

"No, I took it in for lunch. Maybe I should run back out."

"We're fine, Aunt Collette."

"Thanks, sweetie," she said, kicking her shoes off. "I've got scarcely an hour to get ready as it is."

"How could it possibly take you an hour to change your clothes?"

She ruffled my hair and laughed. "You have no idea."

I was going to clue her in about Leesha's hairstyling "skills," but before I could say anything, Holly burst into the house, armed with a big tray of hair goo, make-up, cotton balls and—I had no idea what the other stuff was. "Sorry I'm late," she said. "Is Leesha here yet?"

"Hi, Aunt Holly," Leesha answered from upstairs.

"C'mon, girls," Holly announced. "We have a job to do."

Aunt Collette, Holly and Leesha spent the next forty-five minutes in the bathroom. I don't know what they were doing in there, but I heard a lot of laughing, a little "ouch"-ing, one "don't peek yet!" and a monstrous blow dryer. Finally, they emerged onto the landing, and I'm here to tell you that Aunt Collette belonged on the red carpet. She was wearing a glittery black dress with high heels, her hair was swept dramatically to one side, and her lipstick was hot pink.

"Wow," I called up to her from the living room.

"You like?" she said.

"I like."

"What about you, Remember?" she said to Mem, who was still in my room.

He came to the doorway and froze when he saw her. "Wow."

"It's unanimous then," Holly said proudly. "She's a wow."

"The real test is what TJ thinks," Aunt Collette said.

"You're a shoe-in," Holly assured her. "Come on, let's go downstairs and I'll touch up your nails."

Aunt Collette had a hard time sitting still for the nail painting. When the bell finally rang, she tripped over herself getting to the door. Holly told her to take a deep breath, and she actually sounded calm when she said, "Hey there, TJ." He, of course, simply said, "Wow." After Aunt Collette introduced everybody, she turned on *Jeopardy* to distract Mem, told me the name of the restaurant about twelve times, then ran to the 'fridge to make sure she'd posted her cell phone number. Finally, the lovebirds left, and so did Holly and Leesha. With Alex Trebek working his spell, Mem didn't seem to notice that the house had emptied out.

I felt happy for Aunt Collette, and I think Mem did too—happy enough to let me turn on *Animal Planet Extreme*, the episode about the messiest eaters on earth. We ended up having Girl Scout cookies for supper (Mem likes the Thin Mints and I like the Samoas) and playing a Sorry marathon. From time to time I wondered how Aunt Collette was doing, and every time I thought of her, I was glad not to be in her shoes. What do you talk about over a whole long dinner, not to mention the car ride there and back? What if you realize before the food even comes that you don't like the person—or even worse, that the person doesn't like you?

I don't think my aunt had any of those troubles though. She moseyed into the house around midnight, holding a spray of flowers and smiling at nothing, a funny glaze on her face. "Hey night owl," she said, slipping out of her high heels and joining me on the living room couch, where I'd been lounging since Mem went bed. "How'd it go?"

"I'm supposed to be asking you that," I said.

She touched her bouquet blossoms and rested her head on the back of the sofa. "Do you have any idea how long it's been since I've gone on a date?"

"You had fun, huh?"

"That's the scary part," she said. "I was kind of hoping I wouldn't. Then I could put the whole thing aside and...gee, it's hot in here. Want to go on the porch for a minute, tell me about your night?"

"Sure."

She got us each a bottle of water, and we plunked ourselves on the front steps, leaning against the railing and stretching our legs along the stairs. One breath of the cool, grassy air and I realized how stuffy the house was. It felt good to be outside with the crickets and the stars. The only light on the street was the Dempster's lamppost, shining dismally onto their mailbox. I avoided looking that way.

"So, how did it go anyway?" she asked.

"It went exactly like when you're at the store. We hung out. It was fine. You weren't worried, were you?"

She had to think about that one. "It's just that

I—I didn't know how Remember would take it—you know, me doing this."

"He took it fine."

"Good," she said, setting her bottle on the step. "So...you think I might be able to do this again sometime?"

"Definitely."

"Like this Saturday?"

"Wow, you really like him."

She laughed a laugh that was almost a giggle. "I'll make it up to you. I think I'm going to hire the Butler girl at the store, and then you'll— "

"Will you finally give me the dirt on him?" I interrupted.

"There's no dirt, Johnny. His name is TJ Cappellucci and he's from New Jersey and he's here because he's thinking of putting in a golf course out by the reservoir."

"A golf course, for real? Wait till I tell Mo."

"Now, nothing's certain yet," she insisted. "For one thing, TJ will have to get some zoning changes, and this is a town that doesn't like to change anything. I think we'd still be driving horse-drawn carriages down cobblestone streets if some people had their way. So don't go telling people this is a go yet."

I took a long drink. "Aunt Collette?"

"Uh huh?"

"What if it's not a go?"

She sat up stiffly. "If it's not a go, then he'll have to go back to New Jersey and figure out where he can put a golf course...somewhere else."

Now I understood why Aunt Collette had hoped she wouldn't like TJ. But she did. She most definitely did.

"Now, Al Dempster," she went on, pointing to Dirk the Jerk's house. "He could help TJ out if he wanted. Al's headed up the town board forever, and he could push a zoning variance through in a snap. I've seen him do it for people he likes, and I've seen him block it from people he's ticked at. You know what? I've got half a mind to go over there and ask him for it myself."

Oh no, oh no, oh no! What had I done? I'd gotten Al Dempster's son mad, that's what. Al Dempster, who held the key to TJ's golf course and Aunt Collette's happiness. If Mr. Dempster ever found out what I'd been doing to his mailbox, he'd never help out Aunt Collette, never in a million years. He'd reject a zoning change out of spite, and it would be my fault. All my fault.

I must've let out a groan or something,

because the next thing I knew, Aunt Collette was saying, "You okay, Johnny?"

"Yeah, fine. I'm just beat all of a sudden. Mind if we go in?"

"Not a bit," she said, standing up and heading inside. "If I knew what was good for me, I'd be in bed already myself."

Thank goodness she went straight upstairs and closed the bedroom door behind her. My innards were going to crawl out through my pores if I didn't do something. I had to fix this mess—or at least try to, and right away. After all, Dirk could tell his father about me at any moment—assuming he hadn't already spilled. My mind raced. I needed a plan. But I didn't have one.

Frantically, I slipped into the kitchen for a pen and paper, started writing, then tiptoed outside and stuck the note in Dirk's mailbox. It said: "TRUCE?" That's all. A peace offering. A gesture of goodwill. Tomorrow maybe I could think of something nice to do for him. I had no idea what that would be though, and my stomach hurt as I shot back to the house.

Remember Dippy   121

Chapter 9

I didn't sleep very well that night, and when Aunt Collette woke me the next morning, I felt like I'd only just drifted off. This must be how Niko felt all the time: stressed, guilty, pressured—and exhausted. Aunt Collette, on the other hand, acted as chipper as if she'd slept till noon. It was funny to see Cinderella back in her 7-11 shirt and cap after her princess look last night. But she didn't seem to mind the tumble down the fashion ladder; in fact, she was downright cheery.

"Let's go, sweetie, I'm on the fly," she sang. "It's a beautiful day—enjoy it." And then she practically skipped out of the room.

Usually I pop up as soon as she calls me, but this time I stayed in bed a while, wondering if I'd ruined things for her and TJ. Enjoy the day? How could I, knowing I might have wrecked everyone's dreams? No golf course for TJ (or Mo), no boyfriend for Aunt Collette, no victory over the evil Dirk for me. Could it get any worse? Aunt Collette must've sensed that I was dawdling because she honked her horn right under my window as she pulled out. "All right, all right," I muttered and dragged my sorry self out of bed.

When I got downstairs I didn't see Mem—the TV wasn't even on—but the front door was open. Glancing out, I could see the back of a man sitting on the steps talking with Mem. I pushed the screen, and they both turned around to face me.

"Mr. Boots?" What was my cranky neighbor doing here?

"That's right," he answered, and in a minute his dog, Millie, came barreling from the backyard barking wildly at me, as usual.

"I told you Chip comes to see me," Mem beamed. He reached out his hand for Millie, and she obediently sat at his feet without making a peep.

"I didn't know your name was Chip," I confessed to Mr. Boots.

"My parents named me Chetwin," he chuckled. "With a name like that, you pick up a nickname pretty quick." I'd never heard him laugh before. I'd never even seen him smile, come to think of it. He looked different now, less wrinkled up. I didn't get it.

"Ma almost ran over Millie," Mem said. "Did you hear her blast her horn?"

"Oh, that's why she honked." I looked to the street for Mr. Boots' car, but it wasn't there. "Did you walk all the way over here?"

"Of course. Millie and me, we walk everywhere—when we're both having a good day, right girl? Hey Remember, you got any Twinkies?"

"I'll get them," I said. "I'm kind of in the mood, myself." I found an almost full box in the pantry and brought them out to the porch. I ate mine whole, but Mem and Mr. Boots sucked out the cream and fed the rest to Millie.

"Hey Johnny, guess where Chip was born," Mem said.

"Hull?" Mr. Boots—Chip—has always lived next to me, so I figured he was from here.

"Nope—Paris."

I stopped my Twinkie in mid-air. "Paris? You left Paris for Hull?"

"Not that Paris," Mr. Boots said. "My Pariss—two s's—is a resort town in Western Florida, right on the Gulf Coast."

"Still sounds better than Hull," I shrugged. "How'd you end up here?"

"You really want to know?" He sounded surprised.

"Yeah."

"Me too!" said Mem. "You really want to know? To know?"

"All right then," he said, feeding his second Twinkie shell to Millie. "First off, you should know what my family did for a living. We ran a little bed-and-breakfast called the Pariss Inn right on the beach, hardly a stone's throw from the water. We always made sure our guests had a pleasant stay—good food, comfortable beds, and free rides on our sailboat. That was my job when I got old enough—taking folks up and down the inlet in our day sailer."

"Sweet," I said.

"One day, a family on vacation from Hull, Vermont, asked me to take them around." He smiled up at the sky. "It was a hot, breezy day, perfect for a long leisurely ride. By afternoon's end, I was hopelessly in love with the older daughter."

Wow, so Mr. Boots hadn't always been an old hermit. He was actually young once, sailing boats and flirting with tourist girls. "Wait," I said. "You aren't gonna tell us you gave up ocean sailing and warm winters to follow a girl you only just met?"

"Not immediately, but eventually, yes. Her father was ailing, see, and she wouldn't leave him. So after we got married, I moved up here and got a job driving the ferry back and forth across Lake Champlain. Did it for almost thirty years."

"What was her name?" Mem asked, his face dotted with Twinkie cream.

"Imogene."

"Imogene," Mem said thoughtfully. "Like the park—Imogene Park—where we had the strawberry shortcut?"

"The very same," Mr. Boots said. "They named the park for her. She's the one who convinced the town to put a park there in the first place. She deserved to have her name on it."

"Did you and Imogene have kids?" I asked.

Now Mr. Boots fixed his eyes on his worn shoes. He lifted one foot to make room for an ant that was scurrying along. Then he drew a slow breath and said, "We wanted them, but it didn't happen. So we had dogs instead, sometimes two or three at a shot. Now Millie here, she's the best of the bunch." Millie thumped her tail happily against the step, keeping her post by Mem's side.

"Millie doesn't like me," I said.

"Well, of course she doesn't. You've never once talked to her or rubbed her belly or even smiled at her. Why should she like you?" And he winked at Mem.

"It's just that I— "

"No excuses," Mr. Boots interrupted. "Actions."

Talk about putting me on the spot. Mr. Boots was daring me to touch the beast whose favorite activity was growling and baring its teeth at me. I couldn't think of anything I wanted to do less, but a dare's a dare. So I reached over Mem's lap and put my hand up to Millie's nose, hoping she wouldn't bite. To my amazement, she sniffed my fingers—and licked them! I scratched her between the ears— Mem showed me her favorite spot—and she started wagging her tail. I could hardly believe it.

"She's as true a friend as you'll ever find," Mr. Boots said. "And we all need friends."

"Yup," agreed Mem. "Millie's my best friend. No, no, you are, Chip. Millie's my second best friend. Where does Imogene live now? Can I meet her?"

Mr. Boots rubbed the back of his neck and looked off at nothing. "The thing is, Remember, she was feeling a little dizzy one day—not terrible, but I took her to the hospital just to be safe. The next thing I know, they're putting her in a nursing home. Just temporary, they say, while she gets better. She was gone within the week."

"Gone where?" asked Mem.

"Heaven, I hope," he said.

"But I thought you said she was gonna get better," Mem said.

"I think the nursing home—being in the nursing home—did her in. Some people just aren't cut out for those places. She was one of them, and I think I am too. I'd die just as sure as my Imogene did."

Mem and I looked at each other and then at our Twinkies.

"Anyways, enough of that. I'd best be off if I'm going to get my errands done," Mr. Boots said, pushing himself up off the steps. "Millie, you come with me. Remember, you take care. And Johnny," he tilted his head toward the Dempster's mailbox, "you keep in mind what I said. We all need friends."

I could feel my face turning crimson. "Bye," I said, but I couldn't look him in the eye. I could only hope that Dirk would get my note and take it the right way. Lucky for me, the phone started ringing so I had an excuse to escape.

"Hello?" I said into the phone.

"Is Remember there?" It was a girl's voice.

"Um, who's this?"

"Leesha."

Weird—why was she calling for Mem? Why was she calling at all? "Hold on," I said. "He's just saying good-bye to a neighbor." Hearing the screen door squeak open and slam shut, I called, "Phone's for you."

Mem came running into the kitchen, wide-eyed. I wondered if he'd ever gotten a phone call before.

"It's Leesha," I said, handing him the phone.

Grinning so wide it must have hurt, he grabbed the receiver. "Leesha? Hi, Leesha!" He turned his back to me and started talking in a hush-hush voice, like he was discussing some top-secret project. After a lot of "yups" and laughing snorts, he turned around and said, "Leesha wants to know if I can meet her at Niko's for lunch today. Is that okay, Johnny? Can I?"

A puff of hairspray would've knocked me over. A girl, asking Mem out? I didn't know what to say. What would Aunt Collette say? She wouldn't let him go by himself, that's for certain, but would she let him go even with a chaperone? Was this a date? And while we're at it, how come Mem was the one getting calls from girls?

By now, Mem was bouncing up and down and waving the phone at me. I had to make a decision. "Tell her it's okay, but I'm coming too," I said. Mem nodded and turned his back to me again.

"Noon," he crowed once he'd hung up. "Noon, okay? Noon. Noon!"

Mem and I beat Leesha to Niko's, so we were already settled at our regular table by the window when she got there. She'd taken her braids out, and her black, green and red hair hung in wild locks down her back. She was wearing funeral colors again: a long black skirt with fringe on the bottom, a black tank top, a black choker, and black nail polish. My mom always says black is slimming, but that wasn't working here.

"Hey," she sighed in a dreary voice and plopped into the seat next to Mem.

"Hi, Leesha!" Mem shouted and then flashed that silly grin of his—apparently, that's his M.O. around girls.

"Hey," she said again, propping her chin on her hands and studying some mozzarella crumbs on the table.

"What's wrong?" asked Mem. Funny, she seemed like her normal self to me.

"What makes you think something's wrong?" she asked.

"We learned it in group. At school. If the ends of someone's mouth are turned down, that means something's wrong."

"Oh." She sat back and drew her knees up to her chest. "I might have to go back home to Chicago soon. I hate that place."

"But you told me you were gonna be here all summer," Mem whimpered. "I thought..."

"I thought I was gonna work for my Aunt Holly," she said. "But she says business is slow right now and she can't afford to pay me. I've tried to get other work, but no one's hiring—except the 7-11, but I'm not old enough. And the deal with my dad is, I can only spend the summer here if I have a job. Damn, I don't want to go back."

"What's so bad about Chicago?" I asked. Chicago is a megacity. It's got two baseball teams. The Great Lakes. Places to explore. Things to do. I'd spend my summer there in a heartbeat.

"What's so bad," she bristled, sitting up, "is that my parents live there, and if they're not yelling at each other, they're yelling at me. They hate me."

"No they don't," I said, figuring she was just being melodramatic.

"You have no idea what you're talking about. You so don't get it."

"Then explain."

"Fine." She leaned forward. "They hate me because I survived the car crash and my brother didn't, okay? Before that, before the accident, they treated us both all right. Now that I'm alive and he isn't, they only care about him." She gasped a little then, as if she'd never said those words out loud, as if she'd startled even herself at the sound of them.

As for me, I wanted to slide under the table and crawl away. I mean, what do you say to someone you hardly know when they tell you their darkest secret? Do you try to cheer them up? Do you act all sad and concerned? "Uh..." I started.

"My father doesn't think I see the empty beer bottles he hides in the car trunk. And my mother, well, she hasn't gotten out of her pajamas since it all happened." She brushed the mozzarella crumbs to the floor. "P.S., my friends don't come over anymore. We end up cutting school to spend time together."

"Cut school?" I said. "Can't you just— "

"Yeah, but it's more fun this way."

"Don't you get in trouble?"

"Not if you know how to manage the system. I'm an expert at that these days."

Whoa, no wonder Leesha never smiled. In Chicago, she was living the kind of misery I thought only existed on TV shows. And if she couldn't get a job here in Hull, she was going straight back there. I thought about TJ's golf course and all the summer jobs the construction would have created—including maybe one for Leesha—and I felt horrible. The damage from my stupid mailbox stunts was snowballing. No golf course, no more romance for Aunt Collette, no summer job for Leesha—what next?

"Are you mad or sad?" Mem asked Leesha. "If your mouth is turned down, maybe you're mad and maybe you're sad. That's what we learned. Are you mad at me?"

"No," she said, trying to turn up the corners of her mouth. "I'm mad at the world, but not you."

That seemed to make him feel better. "Let's get mushrooms this time. Do you like mushrooms on your pizza?"

"Hmm? Oh right, pizza. Yeah, sure. That okay with you, Johnny?"

"That okay with you, Johnny?" Mem said. "That okay with you, Johnny?"

So we ordered a large mushroom pie, and while we ate, we talked about how summers should be.

"Summertime should be all about the ocean," Leesha said.

"You go much?" I asked.

"Never been. But I know I'd love it—the water and the sand. First, I'd swim in the waves all morning, then I'd lie on the beach all afternoon and see what the salt and sun would do to my hair color." She sighed longingly and took a bite of pizza. "It would be perfect, wouldn't it, being away from everything, everyone?"

"Not for me," I said. "I'd want to go to a city, where there's stuff to do all day and all night, and you couldn't get bored if you tried. New York, Boston, LA—heck, I'd take Burlington."

"What about you, Mem?" Leesha asked.

"Me?" he said, sounding surprised that anyone cared what he thought.

"Yeah, what would your dream summer be?"

He licked a string of cheese off his lips. "I like it exactly the way it is."

"You're lucky," she said.

"Yup. Hey, what's that?" he asked, pointing at the half-eaten slice of pizza on her paper plate.

"What's what?"

"What's what?" He pointed closer. "It looks like a paper clip."

"That?" she said, sticking her fingers into the cheese. "I think it's just a mushroom...hey, it's a thumbtack." She held it up and declared, "There's a thumbtack in my pizza!" Mem joined in, only louder and longer. "Dumbtack!" he shouted. "There's a dumbtack. Leesha has a dumbtack!"

Poor Niko, I thought. *He must really be losing it.* It's bad enough when he lets an occasional anchovy fall into a pizza, but a thumbtack? Ouch!

Niko came running out, his baseball cap falling off his head, his face white as flour. "I am sorry, very sorry," he said in a hushed voice and scooped up what was left of our pizza. "I make you a fresh pie—no, two fresh ones."

"Niko, it's all right," I said. "We were almost done, anyway. Don't sweat it."

He looked at Leesha, who only shrugged and pushed her plate away. "No charge, then," he said. "No charge next time, either."

I felt a little bit bad about this, knowing he was saving up for a ring and all. "Really, Niko, it's okay."

"He said no charge," Leesha scowled.

"Fine," I said. "Let's just go then."

"Fine," she said. "C'mon, Mem."

Mem shoved a last bite of pizza into his mouth and followed us out.

Leesha had calmed down by the time we reached the sidewalk. "You know what?" she said. "Niko said he wasn't hiring, but maybe he'll change his mind now. Maybe he'll see how he could really use an assistant. To make sure all the sharp objects stay out of the food."

"Forget it, Leesha," I told her. "Niko's not going to be putting anyone on the payroll anytime soon."

"How do you know?"

"Trust me, I know. He's going through a hard time."

"Aren't we all?" She flipped her striped hair over her shoulder and stuck her hands into the pockets of her black skirt. "Anyways, I'm gonna go keep Aunt Holly company at the shop. See you guys."

"See you," I said.

"Bye, Leesha," Mem said. "Wishing you blue skies. Blue skies."

She just waved and walked away.

By the time we got home I felt drained, but the day's surprises weren't over. Dirk the Jerk had answered my note while we were out. That rat, he'd messed with our mailbox in broad daylight. He'd removed the TRY SC from TRY SCOPE—leaving the discarded letters crumpled on the ground—and added an N, so now it read NOPE. Nope to TJ getting a zoning change, nope to Aunt Collette keeping her boyfriend, nope to Mo playing his favorite sport, nope to Leesha getting a job.

No. No way. I wasn't going to let everyone's life get ruined.

"Mem," I said, "go inside and set up a video game. Any one you want. I'll be in in a minute, okay?"

"Okay? Okay, Johnny, but I'm gonna cream you!" he said and ran into the house.

Without exactly thinking it through, I headed across the street. Both cars were in the Dempster's driveway, so Mr. Dempster had to be home, and I was going to talk to him. Never mind that I didn't know whether or not Dirk had snitched on me. No matter that I had no idea what I should say. I needed to do something, and if I couldn't make any progress with Dirk, I'd have to go straight to the big guy.

By the time I was halfway across the street, I started having second thoughts. Well, not second thoughts as much as outright dread and panic. *What if Dirk answers the door? What if I say something to Mr. Dempster that makes things even worse? What if Mem follows me over here and does something stupid?* But I couldn't let any of that stop me from trying to fix what I'd screwed up. I walked faster so I wouldn't have time to change my mind—across the street, past the mailbox, down the driveway, up the front steps, and onto the stoop.

Which is where I heard the yelling. The

Remember Dippy   137

windows must have been open because I could make out every word. A man—it had to be Mr. Dempster— was hollering that he's had it, that this can't go on, that this won't go on, that things are going to change one way or another. No one spoke back to him, so I didn't know whether he was shouting at Dirk or Mrs. Dempster or maybe someone on the phone, but it sounded a lot like the way my parents shrieked at each other before they split—ear-piercing, furious, a little berserk.

I should have beat it as soon as I heard the fighting, but I kind of froze there on the stoop. The next thing I knew, the front door burst open and Mr. Dempster stormed out, all red in the face and sweat rolling down his bald head. He stopped just short of plowing me down.

"What?" he snapped. "What is it?"

Talk about a case of rotten timing. But here we were, and he'd asked me what I wanted, so I decided to give it a try. "Mr. Dempster, I was wondering if I could possibly talk to you about something. Something that's really important to my aunt."

His eyes narrowed. "Who are you?"

"I'm Johnny. My Aunt Collette lives across the street, and— "

"Not now!" he barked, flying past me and marching over to his car. He slammed the door shut and took off down the street with the radio blaring, leaving me pressed against the porch railing with no idea what I'd walked in on.

Now what was I going to do?

Chapter 10

I holed myself up the next few days, thinking about stuff—moping, really—plus we had a cold snap and there was no point going to the lake. I got a postcard my dad sent from Acapulco, the first stop on his Mexican cruise with Kim, saying he couldn't wait for my visit over Labor Day weekend. *Yeah, right.* Leesha came over a couple of times, and Mr. Boots and Millie stopped by on their way downtown one day. But Mo was busy helping his father build their deck, and Reed was getting over an attack of poison ivy, so mostly it was me, Mem, Linguini and Jambalaya kicking around the house, playing video games, and watching The Weather Channel.

Aunt Collette was working even more than usual because her best clerk was on vacation, and she still hadn't hired the Butler girl. When she finally got a day off, TJ asked her to go see the swans over in Lake Swanton. She told me she could take Mem along if I wanted the time off, but it wasn't like I had big plans or anything, so I told her to go ahead and leave him with me. Who knew how much longer TJ would be around anyway, if the zoning thing failed?

TJ was wearing a wild raspberry-colored Hawaiian shirt when he came to pick up Aunt Collette, and she had on an electric-yellow sundress plastered with bright ruby poppies. You practically needed sunglasses to be in the same room with them. Leesha, who'd been hanging out with us all day, told Aunt Collette she looked nice, but I doubt she meant it. How could a girl whose favorite color is black—right down to her toenail polish—really like fluorescent rainbow-wear?

Once TJ and Aunt Collette left, the three of us played a few hands of I Doubt It and had just taken out the Monopoly box when we heard voices on the front steps. I hopped up and found Mo and Reed at the door, each carrying a paper grocery bag in one hand and a 7-11 slushie in the other. Mo's face and arms were seriously sunburned, and Reed's legs were splotched with the scabs from his poison ivy rash. Both of them should've been home applying lotion, but I was glad they came by.

"Hey," I said, opening the door.

"Hey Johnny, Mem," they said, and then they stood there gawking at Leesha. I forgot that they'd never met her. Funny how you think your best friends automatically know everything about you, especially about who your other friends are.

"Guys, this is Leesha," I said. "She's visiting from Chicago. Leesha, this is Mo and Reed."

Leesha, who was stretched out on the living room floor setting up the Monopoly bank, turned to Mem and said, "They need haircuts big time." Mo and Reed shot daggers at me, but I didn't even try to explain. You can't really explain someone like Leesha. Instead, I asked, "What's in the bags?"

Mo drank the last of his slushie in a slurp loud enough to be heard back at the 7-11. "Oh," he said, kicking an imaginary pebble on the floor, "we kinda thought maybe Mem could help us get our video games to the next level."

"Yeah," Reed added. "I'm still stuck in the lagoon in Shipwreck. What do you say, Mem, can you do it?"

"Yup," Mem answered as he helped Leesha sort the play cash. "Right after the Monopoly game."

"But that could take hours," complained Mo.

"You wanna be the dog or the iron?" Mem asked him. "I'm the shoe and Leesha's the battleship."

Mo and Reed rolled their eyes as they sat down to play. Leesha seemed amused by the whole thing. I was just glad to have my buddies back. Plus, I'm a natural at Monopoly. I bought three out of the four railroads right off the bat. Funny, all I kept thinking was how great it would be to have that money for real—so I could buy up all the state quarters and find Jo her American Samoa.

"Is your aunt upstairs?" Mo asked at one point.

"She's not here," I said. "Why?"

"Nothing. Just, she wasn't at the store when we got our slushies, so I figured she must be home, is all."

I told him she had to go out for a while, but Mem blurted out what I was trying to conceal. "She's on a date," he announced.

"No kidding," Mo said. "Who with?"

"Who with? Who with? TJ!" Mem answered.

"Who?"

"Somebody she met," I cut in. "Reed, it's your turn."

Unfortunately, Mem didn't get the hint to end this particular conversation. "Are they gonna get married?" he wanted to know.

I wanted to know too—everyone probably did. Leave it to Mem to say out loud what the rest of us wouldn't. "No. I mean, I don't know," I said. "No one knows—they only just started seeing each other."

"They're cute together," Leesha said.

"Huh?" said Mem.

"That means you can tell they really like each other," she explained. "That's a good sign."

"Can we get back to the game now?" I asked. I didn't want anyone, especially Mem, getting their hopes up about this guy who, for all we knew, would be moving back to New Jersey next week. But everyone's eyes stayed fixed on me, as if I owed them a bigger explanation about my aunt's love life. Thankfully, the doorbell rang again.

It was Jo. Jo was at my door. I couldn't believe it.

"Hi, Johnny." She smiled her perfect smile.

"H-hi. C'mon in."

"Thanks. Patsy just had to walk by Dirk's house, and she just had to have me go with her. They're out there in his driveway, and I'm gonna puke if I have to keep listening to—oh..." She trailed off when she spotted Leesha, who looked up at her and then turned back to the game.

"Jo, this is Leesha," I said. "Holly's her aunt. She's here for the summer."

"Oh. Nice to meet you," Jo said. But she didn't mean it—she was all ice.

"Hi, Jo!" Mem grinned. "We're playing Monopoly. Johnny's the banker!"

"Cool. Listen, Johnny, I came by to tell you something. You know what I heard about Niko? I heard he accidentally cooked a razor blade into somebody's pizza the other day."

"It was a thumbtack, not a blade," Leesha said.

Jo opened her mouth. No words came out, but I knew she wanted to ask Leesha what made her an instant authority on Niko. So I explained, "That was our pizza."

Jo shifted from one foot to the other. "Oh, you went out to lunch...together?"

"Well, yeah. We...yeah."

"Hey Jo," Mem said. "Wanna be the thimble? Johnny's winning."

Still eyeing Leesha she said, "Wouldn't want to cut in. I'm obviously interrupting." She turned sharply toward the door.

"Jo, wait, it's not like that," I said, but she was already closing the door behind her. "I like your nails," I muttered to no one.

"C'mon, Johnny," Mem said. "The game's not over yet."

I slumped onto the couch. "You play. I'm

Remember Dippy   139

done." Done with Monopoly and, from the looks of it, done with Jo. How did I let this happen?

"Hey, I have an idea," Mo brightened. "How about we call it quits on the Monopoly, and Mem, you can help us with our video games for a while?"

After glancing at Leesha, Mem studied his Monopoly shoe, turning it over and over in his fingers. He sighed a long sigh, like he was having trouble making this big decision. Then he drew in a big breath and bellowed, "The game isn't over!" He flipped over the Monopoly board and threw the bank money in the air. "We're playing Monopoly!" he screamed. "You promised! You're a liar! You prommmmmisssssed!"

Mo and Reed scooted back and sat there with their jaws hanging open. Leesha tried to put her arm around Mem, but he batted her away and started rocking back and forth. "We're playing Monopoly," he whimpered to himself. "We're playing Monopoly."

Time to surrender. "That's right," I said, dropping back onto the floor. "The game isn't over and we need to finish it. Right, Mo and Reed?"

They were too stunned to do anything but nod and move back into the circle. While Leesha gathered up the money, I set the board back up...in a way that, with any luck, put me about five minutes away from winning. "Okay, I think this is how the board was when we left off," I lied, and Mem was content again.

Reed went bankrupt first, then Mem, who I invited to team up with me, then Mo and Leesha. "We won!" Mem whooped. "Johnny and me won! We creamed you all! Ha ha! We won!"

"You sure did," said Mo. "Now can we do StarBender?"

"Okay," Mem said, "but you have to clean up the Monopoly game first."

"No sweat," Mo replied, happily gathering up the Community Chest cards, the money and the tokens. "I wanna get to the Orion Nebula."

"The Orion what?" asked Leesha.

"Nebula," said Mem as he set up the GameCube controllers. "That means a nursery where new stars are being born. I learned about it on The Weather Channel. Martin the Meteorologist says you can see the Orion Nebula in the night sky. He says it has 700 stars, but it looks like just one star, and it's in a picture in the sky of someone wearing a sword. Then he wishes you starry nights."

This was probably supposed to be interesting, but I wasn't in the mood for an astronomy lesson so I got up to get a drink. Leesha must not have been in the mood either because she followed me into the kitchen.

"You want anything?" I asked, opening the 'fridge.

"Naw."

I dug out a mini-carton of orange juice and straddled a kitchen chair. She took the seat across from me and started paging through one of Aunt Collette's *People* magazines. I was glad she didn't feel like talking because I needed to sit and figure out some things. *Okay*, I thought, tapping my fingers against the juice carton, *what exactly just happened between Jo and me? Is she jealous of Leesha— and does that mean she likes me, likes me enough to get jealous? Or did she just decide she wasn't interested—that a guy who sits at home playing board games on a Friday night isn't worth bothering with?* If only I knew what Jo was thinking, I'd know what to do—or not do. Girls are impossible to figure out. I took a long swig from the carton.

"That Jo is wound pretty tight," Leesha said without looking up from her magazine.

"I guess."

"Pretty funny, her thinking you and I were on a date or something. Like that would ever happen."

"No kidding."

She squinted at me and raised one harsh eyebrow.

"I mean, you know what I mean," I said.

"Whatever." She rattled a couple of pages, then asked, "So, what's this hard time Niko's supposedly going through anyway?"

"He lost a really important piece of jewelry—a diamond ring. It fell down the vent in his kitchen floor. That's why he's been so touchy."

"And careless."

"More like forgetful."

"Yeah, well, his forgetfulness could've put a hole in my tongue. Or my innards."

My eyes migrated to the holes in her ears. What were there—six pairs?

"Then he'd really have a problem on his hands," she added.

"I think you'd have noticed it in time."

"Maybe. Maybe not." She snapped the magazine shut and pushed her chair back. "Anyway, I'm gonna go say hi to the ferrets." She grabbed a stack of magazines from the table and was gone. Like I said, girls are impossible to figure out.

At least I had a little peace and quiet now. Quiet, anyway. I didn't feel peaceful at all and didn't know if I ever would. Everything I touched these days turned to megaflop. Maybe I would've been better off spending the summer with Dad and

Princess Kim in Maine, where there was less disaster to get into. But no, problems found me wherever I was, and solutions dodged me. I wondered what would go wrong next.

I didn't get a chance to wonder for very long. Suddenly Leesha was running back into the kitchen shouting, "The ferrets!"

I jumped up. "What's wrong?"

"Nothing's wrong. We can use them."

"What for?"

"To get Niko's ring back." She fell into a chair and tucked both legs beneath her. "My brother—I told you he had a ferret—he told me all about this. In the olden days, people used ferrets to run wires through tight spaces. They tied the wires to the ferrets' legs and let them run through pipes and stuff. I bet Mem's little fur balls could cruise Niko's vent easy."

"I don't know, Leesha. I mean, even if the ferrets could navigate the vents, what makes you think they'd bother picking up the ring? It's not like it's food or something."

"Shows what you know about ferrets. They love shiny things—key chains, ribbon, anything. They'll steal it and stash it away like treasure. A piece of jewelry? Irresistible."

SHIRLEY REVA VERNICK

"But it's dark in those pipes. The ring won't shine. Nothing would."

Leesha's cheeks flushed, and she bit her lip hard.

"Nice try though," I offered.

"No, wait, wait. We'll just shine a light for them, that's all. You must have a flashlight around here."

I shrugged.

"Anyway, I've got a penlight in my purse. Niko must have something too. It's fine."

"I don't know," I said.

"Why, what've we got to lose?"

"Mem's beloved ferrets, that's what."

"No way. Ferrets are way too smart to get lost."

Leesha really knew how to apply the pressure, but I still didn't want to get involved. After all, Niko didn't ask us for help, did he? It really wasn't any of our business. But then I remembered what Mr. Boots said about everyone needing friends, and it seemed like Niko didn't have any right now.

"Well?" she asked.

"Okay, look," I said. "How about we research this a little, and then if we still think it could work, I'll ask Mem."

"I'll ask Mem. Where's the computer?"

"Don't have one. But Mo does."

"Fine. Hey everyone," Leesha shouted into the living room. "Pack up your stuff. We're going to Mo's."

And that was that. Mo and Reed gathered up their game discs, and we all piled out the door. Jo and Patsy were still yakking with Dirk, whose dad was yelling at him through the window to quit goofing off and start washing the cars, but none of us said anything to each other.

When we got to Mo's, I turned on The Weather Channel for Mem, and the rest of us crowded into Mo's room to Google ferrets and discuss Leesha's plan. We found out some incredible stuff—like, ferrets ran the video cabling for Princess Diana and Prince Charles' wedding in 1981. During World War II, ferrets ran wires in U.S. airplane wings. And a few years ago, a pet ferret connected the computers at a U.S. missile-warning center by threading wires through crowded 40-foot-long spaces.

"Listen to this," said Leesha. "It says the word ferret comes from the Latin *furonem*, which means thief. 'Your ferret will happily steal anything it can get its paws on. In fact, the term *ferret out* means to search and discover through persistent investigation.' " Then she turned to me and stared.

I thought about how happy Niko would be to get his ring back, to be able to propose to Carmelita and start sleeping at night again. But I also thought about how devastated Mem would be if Linguini or Jambalaya got hurt or stuck in the vents or if they ran away. Fists in my pockets, I paced the room, feeling my friends' eyes on me, wishing for some Magic 8 Ball to give me the right answer.

Finally I said, "Okay, Leesha, you can go talk to Mem. But here's the deal: we're only doing this if he agrees, and we're only using one of his ferrets. Just one. Okay?"

With that, Leesha jumped up and hugged me, right there in front of everyone. She threw her chubby arms around my neck and brushed her cheek against my cheek. Then she jumped back. "Be right back," she said and ran down to the den for Mem.

While we waited, the guys and I took turns playing Snood on Mo's laptop. Everyone in his family has one because his dad sells computers and gets great deals on them. Mo is so lucky. One time when we were camping at Burr Pond, he brought his laptop and we watched *The Thing from the Lake* on DVD three times in a row. As for me, I'll probably be out of college before I can afford a computer of my own.

"You really think this'll work?" Reed asked, lazing on Mo's unmade bed.

"You don't?" I said.

"I don't know. It's a pretty wacky idea."

I couldn't disagree.

"Hey, maybe Niko'll give you a reward if it works," Mo schemed.

"I'm not doing it for a reward. I'm doing it to be a friend."

"Since when is Niko your friend?" he asked.

"Can't a guy do something nice without everyone making a federal case out of it?" But even as I defended myself, I was getting edgy all over again. Maybe Mo and Reed were right. Maybe this was a stupid idea. Maybe we shouldn't be butting into Niko's business in the first place.

"He said yes!" mouthed Leesha, who was suddenly standing at the door, her arm linked through Mem's.

"Is it true, Mem?" I asked.

"Is it true?" he said, looking at Leesha, then his feet—everywhere but at me. "Is it true? I guess so," he said quietly, sounding resigned.

"Hey Mem," I said, "this is your choice. If you want to think it over, go ahead. Or if you want to say no right now, that's okay too. Don't let us decide for you."

"Can it be Linguini?" he gushed. "Jambalaya, she gets scared."

SHIRLEY REVA VERNICK

"Sure, whatever you want," I said. "Are you sure?"

"Nope. Are you sure?"

"Nope," I said. "But it's not my decision. It's yours."

Mem didn't speak for a solid minute. Finally he said, "Can it be Linguini?"

Chapter 11

We all ran back home for Linguini, her travel case, and some flashlights. By the time we carried everything downtown, Niko was just putting the "Sorry, come again" sign in the door. He closes early on Sundays, which was a good thing; this wasn't something you'd want to do with a shop full of customers.

When we told Niko our plan, the first thing he did was laugh—a glum, quiet kind of laugh. "Is crazy," he said. "Will never work—the vents are too old and twisted."

"But— " Leesha started.

"She is cute little rat," he said. "I don't want you should lose her for nothing."

That really got Mem going. He started rocking on his feet and wringing his hands and "oh no"-ing, until Leesha put her arm around him and whispered something in his ear. Then she turned to Niko and glowered, "Linguini isn't a rat. She's a million times smarter."

"Look, you kids are nice to want to help me. I am sorry I talk mean to your animal, your ferret, but you are wasting your time."

"It's our time to waste if we want to," Leesha pointed out. "Just let us try."

Niko must've been too tired—or too desperate—to argue any longer. "Okay, all right," he shrugged. "But listen, all of you. There are vent openings all over the place. Once you send your creature down, she could pop back up anywhere, or nowhere. Be careful you catch her when she comes out...if she comes out. Now excuse me while I empty trash."

This was probably supposed to scare us into changing our minds. It worked on me, and probably on Mem too, but Leesha was already taking Linguini out of the crate. "Okay," she said as Niko walked away, "let's start her down the kitchen vent. Then everyone will need to find an opening and shine a light at it. Come on." She was so sure of herself, we just nodded and followed behind her.

"Mem, you can be the one to launch her, okay?" I said when we got to the kitchen.

"Yup."

We all stood around the vent, and I lifted the grating off, but Mem didn't move. His fingers were frozen around Linguini's little belly.

"It's time, buddy," I said, but he only clutched her closer.

Finally Leesha stepped up. She stroked Linguini with one hand and leaned on Mem's shoulder with the other. "Don't you get it?" she told him. "This is gonna be fun for Linguini. She's gonna get to run around a really cool maze and go on a treasure hunt. It's a ferret's dream come true."

"What if she doesn't come back?" Mem asked.

"Of course she'll come back—she's got you to come back to. And as a little insurance, I threw her squeaky toy into her carryall before we left your house. She'll come running when she hears it."

"Well..." he said uncertainly.

"Do you want me to send her down?" Leesha asked.

Relief washed over Mem's face. "Yup," he said, handing Linguini over. "You do it. You do it for me."

Leesha scooped up the critter and knelt down by the vent. "You're gonna have lots of stories to tell your sister when you get home, you are. Now it's time to play," she said, sending Linguini whiskers-first into the abyss. "Bye, little guy."

"Little girl," Mem corrected her. He stuck his face into the hole in the floor, trying to catch a glimpse of his friend, but Linguini was already out of sight. We could hear her scampering beneath our feet though, and that was reassuring, especially when I told myself it was the sound of playful exploring, not panicked reeling.

"Okay," Leesha said, "everybody find a post."

Mem and I decided to stay there in the kitchen. Leesha guarded the vent near the front door, Mo took the one near the jukebox, and Reed took the bathroom. I got a little worried when I couldn't hear Linguini's footsteps anymore, but then Reed yelled, "Over here."

It dragged on like that for a long time, with us calling to each other whenever we caught the sound of her. I don't know whether Linguini was lost or just having a ball, but she ran in circles around those air tunnels for what seemed like hours. It got harder and harder to sit around and wait. Finally I told Mem to get the toy shark out of the crate. "I think she's been down there long enough, don't you?"

"Yup." His eyes looked tired from staring down the hole.

When Mem handed me the toy, I called out, "All right, everyone. Keep your eyes peeled." I held up the smiling bug-eyed shark and squeezed it a bunch of times.

"C'mon, Linguini," Mem urged, squatting next to the vent. "C'mon, baby." We didn't hear anything, so after a while I pressed the toy even harder. "Right here, Linguini," Mem said over and over in an almost whisper. He looked so miserable, his face all pinched up and red, I wished I'd never listened to Leesha and her bright ideas.

At last, I heard skittering along the pipes. The sound started out faint, then grew louder and still louder, but then it weakened, fading until it disappeared altogether. A full five minutes of silence passed. I couldn't understand, and I tried to convince myself that I still heard Linguini, if only barely. But I didn't. Mem's shallow breathing was the only sound in the room. I squeezed the shark till my fist ached.

"Mem," I began, knowing I owed him an explanation, or at least some comfort. I closed my eyes and swallowed hard, hoping the right words would eke their way out of my throat. "Mem— "

"There!" Mem interrupted. "Th-there!"

As I opened my eyes, Mem was diving toward the vent and Leesha was running in yelling, "Catch her!"

When Mem stood back up, he was clasping Linguini—who had something between her teeth. Something more dirty than sparkly, but definitely something.

"Baby!" Mem squealed, not seeming to notice the object hanging out of her mouth. "Baby baby baaaaaaby."

"It's the ring!" Leesha cried. "Niko, your ring!"

Niko, Mo and Reed dashed in. I coaxed the ring out of Linguini's mouth and handed it to Niko, who stared and stared, like he wasn't sure this was really happening. Then his eyes got a little teary. "*Grazie, grazie infinite*," he said in a shaking voice. "Thank you, everyone. You save Niko."

"Linguini save Niko," Mem glowed.

"That is true," Niko said, scratching Linguini's chin affectionately. "Hey, how about pizza for the house? Niko's treat."

"Linguini loves pizza," Mem said.

"What is her favorite topping?"

"Chocolate!" Mem and I said in unison.

Niko laughed. "That I cannot do. But I will make something *gustoso*."

"Shouldn't you put your ring somewhere safe first?" Leesha suggested.

"*Si*. I have special secret spot. Now go, go get drinks."

We all raided the soda 'fridge and crowded around our favorite table with Linguini happily wrapped around Mem's neck like a fur collar. Niko, meanwhile, outdid himself in the kitchen. He came out with three enormous pies, one topped with mushrooms and onions, another with sausages and fried eggplant, and the third piled high with extra cheese and pepperoni. "This is special pepperoni," he said, cutting the pizzas with his wheel-blade. "From special butcher in Boston. You enjoy—*manga.*"

"Aren't you going to join us?" Leesha asked. "There's plenty, that's for sure."

"Sorry, I have phone call to make," he grinned and hurried back to the kitchen. It was great to see him back to his old jolly self.

Two oversized slices and a Mountain Dew later, I was bursting. Linguini must've been stuffed too, based on how many crusts we fed her. Boy, what a day. If Aunt Collette was having half as much excitement with TJ over in Lake Swanton, she was having a killer time. Thinking about Aunt Collette, I checked the wall clock and realized she was due home soon. "We better split," I said. "It's getting late."

"Let's take a slice home for Jambalaya," Mem said.

"Good idea," said Leesha. She picked a piece of each kind and stacked them on a bed of napkins.

We waved good-bye to Niko, who was still on the phone with Carmelita, and rolled ourselves out the door. Mo and Reed headed left down the sidewalk, while Mem, Leesha and I went right. Our bellies were too full to walk fast, so we took our time going home, Mem holding Linguini tightly to his chest, and Leesha putting the pizza inside the crate for easy carrying.

"We really managed the system that time," Leesha said as we strolled along. "The it'll-cost-you-twenty-thousand-dollars-to-get-your-ten-thousand-dollar-ring-back system."

"I've gotta tell you," I said, "I wasn't sure it was gonna work."

"I was," said Leesha. "I knew she'd find the ring. How about you, Mem?"

Mem nuzzled Linguini. "I knew she'd find the ring all right, but I was afraid she might not come back."

"Wouldn't come back? But she loves you. Animals always come back if they love you."

That made Mem smile. "I bet Jambalaya's worried."

"Not for long," I said. We were on our street now.

"Anyway," Leesha went on, "I sure hope Carmelita says yes when Niko finally pops the question. Who is she anyway?"

I was trying to remember if Niko had told me anything about her, but suddenly someone was racing up behind us on a bike. I jumped out of the way— knocking into Mem—just in time to see Dirk the Jerk swerving and pedaling off. There was no time to say anything to him though, because Linguini freaked at the commotion. She clawed her way out of Mem's arms and tore down his pant leg, then sprinted across the next-door neighbor's yard and on into the bushes.

Mem froze in his tracks, like the day he decided his sneakers didn't fit. "No!" he screamed. "No! No no no no!"

Leesha and I darted after Linguini, but it was getting too dark to see. I pulled the squeaky shark out of my pocket and started squeezing like crazy, but no Linguini. Leesha took a piece of pizza out of the carryall and waved it like a lure, but no Linguini. Mem moaned and rocked and flailed his hands, but no Linguini. We searched and called and squeaked and waved our flashlights for an hour, but still no Linguini.

"She's not coming back, is she?" Mem choked. "Is she? Is she? Is she? IS SHE?" I hoped he was asking Leesha, but he wasn't. He was talking to me.

SHIRLEY REVA VERNICK

"She's just scared right now," I said. "Let's go home and start looking again first thing in the morning. She'll be fine out here overnight."

"Nooooo!" he stamped his feet. "I want Linguini! She's my ferret and I want her!" He stopped hollering and started huffing and puffing, like he'd just sprinted a mile.

"Mem, she's going to be fine," I repeated. "It's summer, it's a warm night, and she'll be fine."

He obviously didn't believe me, but he let Leesha take his arm and lead him in the direction of home. He must have been exhausted, or else he'd still be throwing a fit.

"Who was that fool, anyway?" she asked as we rounded the driveway.

"Dirk Dempster. He lives right over there," I said, pointing to his house.

"He should be out here helping us look," Leesha grumbled.

"No way," I said. "I don't want anything to do with that moron."

"All right. Well, I better go," she said. "Mem, call me tomorrow, and we'll look around."

"Look around what?" he asked.

"Look around for Linguini. Okay?"

"Yup," he said gloomily.

Remember Dippy   159

"See you later," I said and retrieved the carryall from her. The driveway felt long and lonely as we walked up it. "Hey Mem," I said, "let's not tell your mom the bad news about Linguini yet."

He grabbed my arm. "Bad news? You said she's gonna be fine overnight. You said we'll find her tomorrow. You said, you said she's fine."

"Mem, relax. She is fine. What I mean is, let's not tell your mom that Linguini is outside, that's all. She might get a little worried, just like you're a little worried. Why upset her? We'll get Linguini back, and your mom won't even have to know." At least, I hoped we'd get our little hero back. "Do you understand?"

"Do you understand?"

"Mem, come on. Do you understand?"

"Yup," he said, not very convincingly.

"Really?"

"No."

"Well, will you trust me that this is the best way?"

He stared at me blankly for a minute. "I trust you, Johnny," he finally said. "I trust you."

"Good. Now let's get inside."

We beat Aunt Collette back. When she did show up, she was all bubbly and happy—another successful date with TJ. I was relieved and a little surprised that Mem didn't spill the bad news about Linguini—it was hard even for me not to blurt it out. But there didn't seem to be any point in ruining her evening. We'd ruin it tomorrow if we had to.

I lay awake in bed for a long time that night, hating Dirk, feeling sorry for Mem, and worrying about Linguini out there in the big black night. For the first time all summer, I actually heard Jambalaya cry, and I think I heard Mem crying too.

Chapter 12

The minute Aunt Collette left for the store the next morning, Mem and I, armed with binoculars and the squeaky shark, hit the street. Fortunately, Aunt Collette was on the early shift and had to be out of the house before eight. I really didn't want to tell her we'd lost—let's face it, I'd lost—her ferret. With any luck—no, with a truckload of luck—we'd have Linguini back in her cage before Aunt Collette got home, and she'd never have to know.

Luck evaded us. Linguini wasn't anywhere—or if she was, she wasn't interested in letting us know. We paraded up and down the street a hundred times, poking around people's shrubs and gardens, and then we did the same thing on the next street and the one after that. Mem kept getting distracted by anything that caught his eye: a water sprinkler, a squirrel, a spider web, a bird feeder. Maybe that was a good thing—it kept him from panicking over Linguini—but it also slowed us down, like when he got engrossed by a mob of ants swarming around a dropped lollipop. After a couple of fruitless hours, I sent Mem home to watch Martin the Meteorologist and got on my bike to cruise the farther streets. I even rode down to Niko's to see if Linguini had gone back there for more pizza. Dumb, I know, but I was desperate.

When I returned to the house, empty-handed and tired, I found Mem and Leesha sitting on the living room floor playing blackjack while The Weather Channel droned in the background. "I'm sorry," was all I could say.

"Sorry for what?" Mem asked cheerfully.

"For not finding Linguini."

His face fell.

"Maybe she'll come back on her own," I said, dropping onto the sofa. "When she gets hungry. And misses us."

"Miss us?" he said. "But we're right here."

"No, I mean, when she gets homesick."

Mem's eyebrows crumpled together. "She's going to get home sick? Why's she going to be sick when she gets home?"

"No, I—oh never mind."

Leesha picked up the phone by her side and handed it to me. "Mo wants you to call."

"Hey, maybe he found Linguini," Mem perked up.

"No, he doesn't even know she's lost," Leesha reminded him.

I dialed Mo's number and told him about Linguini. He offered to help us search but asked if we wanted to go for a dip at the lake first. Goofing off while Linguini was still MIA didn't seem like the right thing to do...although it sure was getting hot out. Then I had an idea. "Hold on, Mo. Leesha, do ferrets like water?"

"Don't know," she said, shuffling the deck of cards. "But my brother's ferret once jumped into a bubble bath and didn't mind it."

"Okay, Mo," I said. "Meet us at the lake, and we'll scout around for Linguini there. Will it be... just you?"

"I'll invite Jo, if that's what you mean," he said.

Of *course* that's what I meant. "Thanks," I said. "Call Reed too. We need all the eyes we can get."

"We going swimming?" Mem asked when I hung up. "I like swimming."

"A quick swim and a look around. C'mon everyone, let's go."

"I'll wait here," Leesha said.

"Why?" Mem asked.

She fidgeted with her long black skirt, avoiding Mem's eyes. "I don't...I don't have a swimsuit. And I burn easy. Besides, someone should probably stick around in case Johnny's right about Linguini coming home by herself. You go."

I wondered what that was all about, but only for a second. I had other problems to solve.

A bunch of kids, more than usual, were splashing in the water and floating on inner tubes. The lake is really the only place to be when it's this hot. Most people around here don't have air-conditioning in their houses, so if you want to cool off, you have to go to the lake. I doubted Linguini would brave a crowd like this, even if she did want to escape the heat, and I promised myself we wouldn't stay long.

After a few minutes Mo, Jo, Patsy and Reed straggled onto the beach. Jo was wearing a cobalt blue bikini, and she looked amazing. I looked down at my bare chest and arms and decided I needed to start lifting weights.

"Hi, Jo! Hi!" Mem grinned.

"Hi. Hey, I heard about the ring," Jo said when she reached Mem and me. She didn't sound mad anymore; maybe it was because Leesha wasn't with us. "That's great."

"Yeah, Linguini really came through," I said.

"Came through what?" Mem asked. "Through the pipes?"

"Yeah," I said. "Exactly."

"I could've helped, you know," Jo said.

"I thought you were, you know," I stumbled. "You seemed kind of mad. But you can help us find Linguini now if you want. Did you hear she ran off when— "

Jo wasn't really listening anymore—she was gazing off somewhere behind me. I turned around to see what the fascination was. It was Dirk. He sauntered our way, nodded to Jo, and stopped in front of Patsy, who was sitting on her towel applying sunblock. "Hey Patsy," he said, flashing his teeth at her.

"Gotta go," Jo said to us.

"Jo," I called when she was already halfway back to Patsy, then I caught up with her. I wanted to tell her she could hang out with us. That Dirk was a fool. That Patsy didn't need a wingman. That she was allowed to have her own fun. What I ended up saying was, "I like your nails."

"Thanks," she smiled. "Well, see ya."

I stood there for a minute, unsure of what had just happened between Jo and me. I mean, one minute she wants to talk, and the next minute she's running off. Was I missing something here? Saying the wrong things? Not saying the right things?

"You going in?" I heard Patsy ask Dirk.

"Uh huh," he said. "I'm training for the Habitat for Humanity triathlon over in Wilston. I'm gonna swim across the bay and back now."

"Across the bay? That's gotta be half a mile each way. How can you do that?" Patsy asked, all syrup and smiles.

"Easy. Every time I kick, I pretend it's my father's head. Same trick I use when I'm dribbling a ball. Wanna come?"

"I don't think so. We're landlubbers, right, Jo?"

"Okay," he said, "maybe I'll see you on the flip side then."

I thought Dirk was selling Jo and Patsy a story. Really, Dirk Dempster doing a fundraising event for charity? No way. Besides, Dirk might be a star on the basketball court, but he was no big swimmer. He was snookering the girls into thinking he was some kind of ironman. So I kept an eye on him, figuring he'd wait till we weren't looking and then split for the hammock in his backyard. Even when he walked straight into the water and swam away, I assumed it was part of an act. But when he got out so far he disappeared from sight, I decided he was really going to do it. What a show-off. All he wanted was an audience. Well, what I wanted to know was, what gave him the right to spend the day impressing the girls when Linguini was still missing? This was his fault, and he should've been helping us look for her.

At that point Mo was calling out, "Last one in's a rotten golf ball!"

Mo was right—it was time to get wet. Mem and I threw down our towels and ran with Mo and Reed into the water, which wasn't as frigid as it was the last time but was still plenty cold. Jo eventually came in up to her knees but only lasted a few minutes. After about half an hour of water war, handstand contests, and nerf catch with the guys (Mem mostly just watched and splashed around), we were all starting to lose the feeling in our feet, so we raced for our sun-toasted towels.

"Let's lie out for a while," Patsy said as the rest of us dried off.

"You just did lie out," Mo said. "You want to wait around for Dirky Boy to get back, that's all."

"Do not," she insisted. "He'll be gone for hours. I just like it out here."

"I'll hang with you," Jo said.

"No way," said Mo. "You promised you'd help look for Linguini. This is an all-hands-on-deck situation."

Way to go, Mo, I thought. Searching for Linguini was about to get a lot more interesting. Heck, doing dishes would be interesting as long as Jo was there.

Patsy frowned over her sunglass rims and whined, "Jooooo."

"It's the only way he'll let me use his sleeping bag next week," Jo said. "You do want to go camping, don't you?"

I watched Patsy staring down Jo and Jo looking torn, and I knew what I had to do. "Never mind about Mo," I told Jo. "You can use my sleeping bag, no strings. We'll be all right without you."

Jo seemed surprised. She peered at me with a half smile and a look of...something. "C'mon," she said to Patsy, "it's starting to cloud up, anyway. Let's find the ferret."

Sweet. Maybe there was hope for Jo and me yet.

"Let's find the ferret! Let's find the ferret!" Mem hooted, marching in place. "The ferret!"

"Fine," Patsy sighed, pushing her shades back up her nose. And so it was settled.

After all that negotiating, it only took us a few minutes to scour the beach, where the only critters were a couple of seagulls, so we tied our towels around our waists and walked barefoot back to the house. Mem, eager to see if Linguini had made it home by herself, ran ahead of us. I started thinking about whether it was worth losing Linguini to get Niko's ring back. Then I remembered that it wasn't Niko's ring that did this; it was Dirk. I wanted to tell Patsy she was crazy to give him the time of day. I wanted to tell Jo to stop wasting her time with the two of them. But I didn't. I just kept walking.

When we got to the house, we found Leesha sitting on the porch steps eating an orange Popsicle while The Weather Channel hummed through the screen door.

"I've brought reinforcements," I said. "Now we can spread out."

Leesha wiped an orange drip off her chin. "Dirk's the one who should be spreading out. What's his problem, anyway?"

Patsy's eyes narrowed. "For your information, Dirk's in training, and right now he's swimming across the bay."

Leesha rolled her eyes.

"Hey," I said, "you two haven't even met. Leesha, this is Patsy. She's Dirk's friend."

"Friend?" Leesha said. "You actually talk to that, that..."

"That what?" Patsy demanded.

I was afraid this was going to turn really nasty, but then Mem appeared in the doorway and interrupted the skirmish.

"That's bad," he said through the screen.

"What's bad?" Leesha asked.

"Dirk. Swimming. There's gonna be a storm. Unexpected strong winds moving in quickly from the Northeast, bringing torrential rains and severe lightning, with flash flooding in low-lying areas," he quoted The Weather Channel. "Dangerous riptides may develop. Marty the Meteorologist says stay away from water when there's lightning, or you could get hurt."

Torrential rain? Severe lightning? Riptides? Dirk was probably in the middle of the bay by now. Even if he noticed the sky turning, he might not be able to get to shore in time, especially if he got caught in a riptide. He was a jerk all right, but we'd be even bigger jerks if we didn't do something to help him. He could die out there.

The first roll of thunder boomed overhead. Mem practically jumped into my arms.

None of us said anything for a long moment. Finally Patsy moaned, "No—oh no, it can't storm. It can't." Jo hugged her then.

"All right, let's not just stand here," I said. "I'll run over and tell his parents."

"No," Patsy said. "His dad's out of town somewhere, and his mom's at work."

"Well, where does she work?" I asked.

"I, I don't even know," she spluttered. "I just don't—wait, Dirk said she works at a—I don't know—an art supply store or something. In Potsdam."

"All the way up there?" I said. "That's forty-five minutes away."

Everyone started talking at once until Leesha, who had the loudest mouth in the group, shouted, "Stop it! We're wasting time. Someone needs to call the police."

That seemed obvious once she said it, so I ran inside and called 911 for the first time in my life. The dispatcher asked me a hundred questions. I couldn't answer most of them—like, where to reach Dirk's parents. But I did know the exact point Dirk started from and the approximate time he set out, which the dispatcher said was helpful. I gave him Dirk's address and my name and a bunch of other information, and he said they'd get a rescue crew right out. As I hung up, a jagged streak of lightning flashed past the window.

Before we knew it, the rain hit. The lightning grew dazzlingly bright, the thunder ear-splittingly close. We huddled around the kitchen table, listening to the powerful sounds outside, wondering about Dirk and about Linguini too. Patsy stared unblinking out the window at the thick daggers of electricity ripping the sky. We all knew what she was picturing, and there was nothing we could say to make it better, so we didn't say anything. Mem sat rigid in his chair, his hands twitching frantically, as if each finger had a life of its own. "Torrential rains and severe lightning, flash flooding and dangerous riptides," he muttered again and again. I wanted to divert him from his worries, but it was pointless. Our imaginations were raging like the storm.

Finally, Mem's hands stopped twitching. He pushed back his chair, stood up and, without a word, started walking out of the room.

"No, Mem, no disappearing," I said. "Not today."

"I'm just gonna check on Jambalaya," he replied. "Thunder scares her...scares them both."

"I'll go with you," Leesha said and followed him upstairs.

The rest of us stayed at the table for a while, but the silence between us was suffocating, so I said, "C'mon, let's turn on the TV." We went to the living room and tried watching Pet Star, but the storm had ruined the reception. Instead, Mo and Reed settled into an Air Angler match, and Jo and Patsy sank like stones on the couch while I tried to lose myself in a magazine. We must have looked like a bunch of grim statues when Aunt Collette unexpectedly walked in a while later, dripping with rain.

"Aunt Collette, what are you doing home?" I asked.

"Remember called," she said. "Come on, we're going to the lake. I can take up to five of you."

"The lake—why?" I asked.

"I don't know," she said, pulling off her drenched sweatshirt. "I just feel like that boy should have someone there, someone who isn't a total stranger. And if his folks can't be there, I will. Now, who's coming?"

I wasn't sure that made sense, and yet it seemed like a good idea. Mo and Reed volunteered to stay behind, so Mem, Jo, Patsy, Leesha and I crowded into the car and, with the wipers beating a breakneck rhythm on the windshield, made our way to the lake. A fire truck and an ambulance were parked there, and we could just make out the rescue boat on the lake. Aunt Collette turned off the car and squinted out the window.

"Now what?" Leesha asked.

"Now we wait," said Aunt Collette.

"I hate waiting," said Mem.

"Me too," I said. I'd never seen the lake this rough—choppy, churning—or this black. The whole sky ignited with the lightning. The rain pelted the car so hard it muffled the thunder. What if Dirk couldn't stay afloat out there? What if he got struck by a zillion volts of electricity?

After a while, Aunt Collette turned on one of her Dixie Chicks CDs. Every song felt like an hour, and the next hour felt like a week. Then something happened.

The rescue boat stopped. A man in a wetsuit jumped out of it. We lost sight of him in the waves, so we couldn't tell what he was doing. All of us pressed against our windows, but it was no use—we couldn't see what was going on, not until he climbed back onto the boat with the help of the other man on board.

"He-he's alone," Patsy spoke just loud enough to hear. "Why is he alone?"

Remember Dippy   175

No one answered her.

"If he went into the water, he must have spotted Dirk," Patsy said frantically. "Why doesn't he have Dirk?"

"Wait, look," said Jo, pointing out the window. "They're leaning over the bow. They're pulling on something. A rope."

Hand over hand, the men dragged on the rope. Finally, we could see that there was a person on the other end of it, a person who had to be Dirk. The men hoisted the drooping body onto the boat and lay it on the deck. Then they knelt down, and we couldn't see any of them any more. Patsy started to cry, and so did Jo.

Mem cleared his throat and asked, "Is he...?"

...dead? Could Dirk Dempster be dead? It didn't seem possible. I saw him alive just a few hours ago. People aren't supposed to die before they get to high school. They're supposed to live long enough to get their first car, travel the world, have grandkids. They're supposed to be old and crotchety when they die. Not young. Not my age.

"I don't know, sweetheart," Aunt Collette told Mem.

"They might be doing CPR or something on him."

"CP what?" he asked.

"They might be trying to help him breath, is what I mean," she said. "We'll just have to wait and see."

"I hate waiting," Mem said.

We didn't have to wait long. In a few minutes, the boat started moving toward shore, and as it did, one of the men helped Dirk sit up.

He was all right!

Patsy burst into harder tears, and we all cheered. I never thought I'd be so happy—or happy at all—to see Dirk, but I was, and, funny thing, I somehow couldn't wait to tell Mr. Boots all about it.

"I think we've just witnessed a miracle," said Aunt Collette, starting the car back up. "Come on, let's go home."

We were all back in the living room, all except for Aunt Collette, who went back to work, when a police cruiser turned into the Dempsters' driveway. We crowded around the window just in time to see the back door open and a bare foot poke out. The foot was attached to a soaked, slumped Dirk Dempster. Sluggishly, the rest of his body emerged. He was wrapped in so many blankets he could barely move, but he was moving.

Two cops escorted Dirk inside his house and

Remember Dippy   177

stayed with him until Mrs. Dempster pulled in about twenty minutes later, at which point the storm was lifting. She screeched into the driveway, and when she shot out of her car, all we could see was a yellow streak as she hurtled into the house in her rain slicker.

"I wonder if his parents know about his lake-swimming habit," Mo said.

"I wonder if he's ever even tried it before," pondered Reed. "I bet he was just showing off."

"I wonder what his parents are gonna do to him," I said. "My mom would strangle me."

Patsy shuddered.

"What I wonder," said Leesha, her forehead pressed against the window, "is if Dirk'll ever find out."

"Find out what?" I asked.

She pinched her lips together. "That we're the ones who got him rescued. That Mem's the one who figured out he was in danger."

Wow, now there was a good point. I didn't care one way or the other whether Dirk himself found out, but I definitely wanted his dad to know. That would be TJ's ticket to a zoning variance—and to staying in Hull! I had to make sure Mr. Dempster learned about Mem's heroics, and if that meant telling him myself, I would. I'd do anything to make Mr. Dempster realize he owed us a big favor.

As I thought my happy thoughts, I noticed Mem gazing glumly out the window. I knew what he was thinking: Linguini had never felt a raindrop in her life, much less a storm like this. "Anyone want to try the TV again?" I asked in a last-ditch effort to distract him.

"How about the shopping network?" Mem suggested.

"I didn't know you watched that," I said.

"Don't. But tired of the weather today."

"Don't worry," I said. "The storm's over. Things are looking up. It'll be okay."

He gazed at me like he wasn't sure I was telling the truth. I wasn't sure either. I mean, could we really expect a second miracle? More wait and see, I guess.

Chapter 13

Things nose-dived later that night. My bedroom
ceiling sprung a pack of leaks from the rain. I woke
up around 3:00 a.m. to a waterlogged blanket and
the spatter of water dripping on my duffle bag. I
padded across the soggy rug and trudged downstairs
to try to get some shut-eye on the couch, but Aunt
Collette had beat me there so I ended up on the
living room floor. Needless to say, I didn't get much
sleep. When Mem came down at the crack of dawn
and turned on the TV, I crawled into his bed until
Aunt Collette had to leave for work.

The rest of the day was pretty wretched too.
Mem and I traipsed up and down the drizzly, worm-
strewn street a thousand times calling for Linguini.
Every time we passed Dirk's house, I wanted to

pound on his door and tell him to get out here and help us. He owed it to us, to Linguini, to Mem.

To top it all off, Leesha stopped by in the afternoon with more bad news. Mem and I were playing Olympiad when she showed up wearing ebony rhinestone sunglasses that I soon realized were meant to hide her puffy, bloodshot eyes. "It's official," she muttered, squeezing her six feet in between Mem and me on the couch. "My summer's over."

"Huh?" said Mem, studying her black high-heeled sneakers. "Summer's over? It's gonna get cold?"

"No, it's not gonna get cold yet. But I'm going home on Sunday."

"What?" he cried. "Sunday? Why?"

She sniffled and lifted her shades long enough to rub her eyes. "Because I don't have a job, that's why."

"But, but," Mem faltered, "you can still find one. We'll help you find one. Right, Johnny? Leesha has to stay. Here. Right, Johnny? We'll find Leesha a job, right?"

Leesha put her arm around his shoulder. "Thanks Mem, but my parents already bought the airplane ticket so unless you can find me a job in the next three days, I'm history."

What rotten luck. "Are you sure you've tried everywhere?" I asked.

"I even went back to Niko's, hoping he might feel, you know, obligated," she sighed. "You were right, Johnny. He can't afford it. But I did find out Carmelita said yes. Nice to know somebody's life is going right."

"That's not fair!" Mem howled and started stamping his feet. "I won't let you go! It's not fair! It's not fairrrrrrr!" On the last "not fair" he picked up his GameCube controller and hurled it at the entertainment center. It hit a framed baby photo of Mem, shattering the glass.

"Mem!" I yelled, and he knew I was mad. He started whimpering that he didn't mean it, he was sorry, he didn't mean it. "Mem, calm down," I ordered. "It's not that big a deal. I'll clean it up."

"I'll clean it up," he said. I thought he was just parroting me, but then he went over to the entertainment center and started picking up the glass shards with clumsy motions of his bare hands.

"Mem, stop!" Leesha and I said at the same time.

"I'm sorry," he moaned. "I'm sorry."

"I'm sorry too," Leesha told him, leading him away from the glass. "Sorry I brought bad news.

Sorry it made you upset. But hey, we can always hope for a miracle, right? A blue skies and starry nights miracle, for me."

Mem did a double take when he heard Leesha quoting Martin the Meteorologist. "Yeah," he said dreamily, "maybe a miracle. A blue sky miracle. For you. For Linguini. Hey, we should go out and call for her again. Wanna help us?"

"Can't. Aunt Holly took the afternoon off because, well, the shop's dead, and she wants me to mind the phone. Hey, why don't you guys keep me company?"

Mem drew his shoulders up to his ears and let them fall limply back into position. He didn't want to leave his ferret vigil, but I, for one, needed a change of scenery, and as long as Leesha wasn't going to touch my hair, I was up for helping her babysit the shop.

"C'mon, Mem," I coaxed. "We'll stop by the store and visit your mom too."

I kept trying to talk him into it while I cleaned up the glass. He finally agreed, and that's how we wound up spending the next few hours at Hair by Holly. The phone didn't ring once, but Holly had some decent magazines and a deck of cards, and I got us some slushies at the 7-11 after I crushed everyone at Go Fish.

When Holly returned to lock up the shop, Mem and I caught a ride home with Aunt Collette, and, after a late spaghetti supper, I put dry sheets on my bed and slept like a log all night.

To my surprise, I was the first one up the next morning—I guess that's what ten straight hours of sleep will do for you—and that's when I first noticed it. I was sitting on the front steps eating cereal out of the box when my eye caught our mailbox. The letters used to spell NOPE, but now they spelled—I had to squint and shade my eyes from the sun for a minute—they spelled OPEN. Someone—it had to be Dirk—had rearranged the letters and apparently wanted me to open up the mailbox.

As I walked toward the box, I realized the door was already pried open a little. Memories of mouthwash gurgled through my mind. *Here we go again*, I thought, pulling the door gingerly, not knowing whether I was going to find a thank-you note or a dumb prank inside. It was neither.

It was Linguini!

Her shiny brown eyes glimmered at me from the darkness of the box, and I think she was actually smiling. I know I was. She was standing on a pile of what looked like confetti, and some of the confetti fell to the ground as I scooped her up and locked her in my arms. I checked her over for cuts or bites or other injuries, and she seemed fine—thin but fine. I couldn't believe it. And I couldn't wait to tell Mem.

Then a dark thought struck me. How did Dirk get Linguini anyway, and how long had he been holding onto her? Maybe he'd found her outside yesterday or the day before and kidnapped her. Maybe that's why we couldn't find her ourselves. Maybe he was going to keep her forever, except his parents said no or it was too much work or he decided to go honest after getting a second chance at life. What other explanation could there be?

I decided not to tell Mem my suspicions. Let him be happy to get his pet back. I'd figure out some way to deal with Dirk on my own. I ran inside and tiptoed upstairs into Mem's room—he was lying on his back snoring lightly—and set Linguini on his chest. He must've been out cold because he didn't move a muscle as Linguini stepped onto his pillow and curled up in a ball next to his ear. I left them that way, figuring the one would wake the other soon enough.

Soon enough happened a half-hour later, and I knew it because Mem screamed at the top of his lungs, "Linguini! Linguini, you're back! I thought you'd never come back! Blue skies! It's a blue sky miracle!"

I raced upstairs to tell him to lose the theatrics—
Aunt Collette still didn't know Linguini had been
missing—but she got there first. "Remember, honey,
what's wrong?" she asked urgently.

"I felt something against my face," he glowed,
"and it was Linguini! She was in my bed."

"Now, how many times have I told you not
to take those ferrets to bed with you?" she scolded.
"We're going to end up losing them that way."

"But Ma, I— "

"It's my fault, Aunt Collette," I cut in before
Mem could give our secret away. "I brought her into
my bed. She must've climbed into Mem's room in the
middle of the night. I won't do it again."

"Good," she said. "Now that that's straightened
out, I have to get ready for work." She started toward
the door, then turned around. "But I'm taking the
weekend off for a change. You boys feel like going up
to Sugar Loaf? TJ wants to see it."

"Sounds great," I answered. Mem was too busy
smothering Linguini with kisses to say anything, so I
added, "Ditto for Mem."

With Linguini safe at home, the Dippy family was
complete again. Mem's funk dissolved, and Aunt
Collette never had to know about the ferret fiasco.

What a relief. When it got to be a decent hour, Mem called Leesha, who said we should celebrate the good news over lunch at Niko's. I left a message on Reed's voicemail, then called Mo's house. Jo answered the phone.

"Hello?" she said.

"Jo, hi, it's Johnny. Guess what—Linguini's back."

"Hey Mo, the ferret's home," I heard her say. "That's great, Johnny. Thanks for letting us know."

"We're going to Niko's for lunch if you, y'know, want to come."

"Hold on. Patsy, do you want to— " Jo must have put her hand over the receiver then, because her voice got muffled. Then she came back on. "Sounds good. Around noon?"

"Sure. You'll tell Mo?"

"He can't. He's got to work on the deck with our dad, and Patsy's going home, so it'll just be me, I guess. See ya."

Sweet. "See ya."

The only thing still nagging at me now was the Dirk factor. Who did he think he was, stealing a living thing? I didn't care if he almost drowned—he was still a jerk. Did he even know that Mem had probably saved his life? As the morning dragged on,

I got madder and madder, until I realized what I had to do. Before I could go to Niko's or anywhere else, I had to settle things with Dirk. Face to face. I had to—for Mem and Linguini's sake, for Aunt Collette and TJ's sake, and yes, for my sake too.

As soon as I rang Dirk's bell, I wanted to abort the mission, but I didn't get the chance. He opened the door so fast I got the feeling he'd been watching me out the window. Now he was standing in the doorway, a head taller and a lot broader than me. I took a step back, wondering how fast I could run if I needed to.

We watched each other without a word. Dirk's skin was pale, which made his freckles look an even brighter shade of orange, and his nose looked like he'd blown it all night. Served him right. He could've ended up with a lot worse than a head cold, that's for sure.

I inspected Dirk's eyes, hoping to locate a trace of regret or gratitude or embarrassment—something that would give me the confidence to say what I'd come to tell him. But there was nothing. His whole face was a blank. Who knows, maybe his whole personality was a blank, a big empty nothing, in which case it would be futile to talk to him. I was ready to cut my losses and scram, but then he spoke.

"Hi," he said in a froggy voice. Funny, he'd never said that word to me before, that simple word friends always use. It threw me off guard.

"H-hi," I stammered. "Listen, Dirk—"

"C'mon in. The teapot's whistling."

Had Dirk the Jerk actually invited me into his house? Maybe this was a trick. Or maybe aliens had abducted the real Dirk and replaced him with a look-alike who knew some manners. I took one step through the doorway and hesitated, but Dirk was already walking down the hall, assuming I'd follow, so I did.

In the kitchen, Dirk had lined up a mug, a tin of tea, a lemon, and a jar of honey. Apparently, he knew my grandmother's remedy for whatever ails you. "You sick?" I asked.

"Getting better," he coughed. "At least I can talk now." He poured the hot water, then scooped the loose tea leaves into a strainer and dropped it into the mug. "The lemon and the honey, they really work."

"Yeah, I know."

"Want some?" he asked, stirring the honey ball into his drink.

"No thanks." This was weird—he was actually being polite to me. "Listen Dirk, I need to talk to you about something."

"Might as well sit then," he said. He hopped onto a nearby stool and put his bare feet up on the kitchen island, which was covered with video games, a pile of colored paper, and a slew of pens. "Shoot."

I decided to stay standing. "It's about my cousin's ferret—what did you do with her, anyway?"

"What are you talking about?" he croaked.

"C'mon Dirk, you put Linguini in our mailbox this morning. How'd you get a hold of her?" I couldn't believe he was going to deny the whole thing. What an idiot.

"I didn't put any ferret in your mailbox. I didn't even know you had a ferret."

The blood rushed to my cheeks in hot waves. "Didn't you see Mem carrying Linguini the other night? When you practically plowed us down with your bike?"

"What? No. No way." He started sipping his tea and coughing again, and I had to admit he looked genuinely mystified. "Sorry about that, by the way, about not looking where I was going. I was just, I don't know, blowing off some steam."

"Steam? You mean, because of me?"

He let out a little snort. "Sorry to disappoint you, Johnny, but you're the least of my troubles. It's my parents. Screaming all the time. At each other.

At me. Sometimes they're both screaming at me at once, but for different things. Drives me bonkers."

Well, there was something I could relate to. My parents were at each other's throats—and mine—for at least a year before they separated. "Are they going to split?" I asked.

"Don't know," he shrugged. "Sometimes I think they're on the brink of it, and sometimes I think they're working it out. I wish they'd just make up their minds already."

"Been there."

"Yeah...so what's this about your ferret?" he asked.

"It's just," I shifted my weight to my other foot, "aren't you the one who wrote OPEN on our mailbox?"

"Yeah..."

"But you say you didn't put anything in the mailbox?"

"Sure I did," he said, slapping his mug on the counter. "I put two notes in there, one from me and one from my mom. To...say thanks...for, you know, helping me the other day."

"Oh..."

Dirk pointed to the stationery on the counter. "We used this stuff from my mom's art store—cotton paper and scented pens. Didn't you get the notes?"

"Uh…" I stepped closer to the counter and ran my hand over the pile of paper. It didn't feel like cotton to me, but it did feel fancy. Then I uncapped one of the pens, a red one, and sniffed it: cherry. The green, purple and black ones were marked lime, grape and licorice. There must have been two or three dozen of them. I picked up the brown one and inhaled: chocolate. "Is this the pen you used?" I asked.

"Hmm? Yeah, I think so. Why?"

I burst out laughing. *Chocolate.* Now it all computed.

"So you didn't get the notes?" he asked.

"No, but I know who did. Linguini. She loves chocolate." I pulled up a stool. "Your note lured Mem's ferret back."

Dirk studied his lap. "I guess I owed you guys the favor."

"How'd you know it was us—the cops tell you?"

"No, Patsy did."

"Oh. Hey, did you tell your dad yet?"

"That I nearly drowned? Yeah, I think it came up in conversation."

"No, I mean, did you tell him about us—about Mem and me—making the call for help?"

Dirk repositioned his feet on the counter and crossed his arms. I couldn't tell whether my question annoyed or amused him. "My mom might've mentioned it to him. Why, you worried about getting credit?"

"No, that's not it, not exactly. It's just that, well, my Aunt Collette might be asking your dad for a favor of her own soon."

"Oh." He uncrossed his arms. "Well, he's been away on business all week, but he's coming home tomorrow."

"Cool."

It seemed like there should be something more to say, but I didn't know what. After all, I'd accomplished my mission. The Linguini mystery was solved, and Dirk's family knew they owed Mem's family. So that was that. Dirk and I could go our separate ways—out of each other's faces and each other's mailboxes. We never had to talk to each other again.

I stood up to leave. "Well, I guess I'll—"

Dirk nodded, "Later."

I turned to go, but I kept hearing Mr. Boots' words. "You have StarBender?" I asked, pointing to the stack of video games on the island.

"Both versions."

"What level you at?"

"Nine. I can't get past that black hole to save my life."

"Y'know, Mem's a wiz at it. He got my Star-Bender to level 12 and my Olympiad to the decathlon."

"Mem did?"

"Yup, and he did the same for Mo and Reed. If you want to bring over your memory card sometime…"

Dirk swallowed a long drink of tea as he thought over the proposition. "Yeah. Maybe."

Then I heard myself saying something that didn't seem to come from my own brain. "Hey," the words started, "some of us are going to Niko's for lunch. You wanna come?"

Dirk looked as surprised as I was. "Can't," he said. "I'm grounded for three weeks."

"Ouch."

He carried his mug to the sink. "Tell me about it."

"Well, there'll still be some summer left when you're freed, so…"

"Yeah, save me some pizza, will ya?"

Dirk walked me to the door, and as I stepped out, I said, "I gotta say, Dirk, I'm impressed. Your mom's at work, your dad's away, no one would have to find out, and you're still toeing the line."

"Don't get too impressed. My mother calls me every twenty minutes. In fact, she's due right about now. Anyway, see ya."

"Yup," I said. "Oh, and Dirk?"

"Yeah?"

"I hope things work out with your parents. One way or the other, I mean."

"Thanks."

Wow, Dirk Dempster said thanks twice in one day. Not bad.

Chapter 14

Fixing things with Dirk unraveled such a tight knot
in my stomach that by the time I walked across
the street and into the house to get Mem, I was
ravenous. Fortunately, it was almost time to meet
Jo at Niko's. I ran upstairs to comb my hair, and we
were about to head out when someone knocked—no,
more like scratched—on the front door. Mem arrived
first and found Millie with her front paws pressed
against the screen, her tail wagging so hard her
whole body shook. "Hiya, Millie!" Mem said, opening
the door and stepping onto the porch. "Hey, where's
Mr. Boots? Johnny, Millie's here but Mr. Boots isn't.
I think she ran away."

"Does she ever do that?"

"Nope."

"Well, let's get her in and call Mr. Boots before he gets worried." I gripped Millie's collar so I could lead her inside, but she wouldn't budge. She woofed urgently, her ears perked and twitching, and then she tried to run down the front steps. "Okay, have it your way," I said. "Mem, you watch her out here. I'll call Mr. Boots. We don't have much time."

No one answered at Mr. Boots', and he doesn't have voicemail. Ratfinks. I didn't want Millie following us downtown, but I didn't want to sit around waiting for Mr. Boots to get home either. I ran outside to see what Mem wanted to do, and that's when I saw what a lather Millie had worked herself into—barking and yelping and practically dragging Mem to the street.

Something was wrong.

"Mem," I shouted over the racket, "I think Millie wants to take us to Mr. Boots."

Mem stopped pulling on Millie. "Then we got to go."

"I'll go," I said, heading for my bike in the garage. "You stay here, okay?"

"No!" he said fiercely. "Mr. Boots is my best friend. I can run there."

"Not in flip flops, you can't. Hold on." I got my bike out of the garage and pulled it into the driveway. "Here," I said, straddling the bike. "You sit on the seat, behind me. I'll pedal standing up."

"But what about Millie?" he asked as he climbed on.

"Don't worry—she'll lead the way."

For an old dog, Millie sure could run. She cut her corners short, jumped a pothole, and darted in front of two cars. With the extra weight I was lugging, it wasn't easy keeping up.

"Where's she taking us?" Mem shouted in my ear as we turned a sharp corner.

I was wondering the same thing. Maybe Mr. Boots fell—or collapsed—while he was out walking Millie. Maybe we were about to find him sprawled on the roadside. But I couldn't tell Mem that, so I just shrugged.

In the end, Millie led us all the way to my house—mine and Mr. Boots'—and tore into the backyard. Mem jumped off the bike and chased after her before I even came to a full stop. I let the bike fall to the ground and ran after him. When we got to the backyard though, Millie wasn't there.

"Millie?" Mem hollered. "Millie girl?"

An eerie stillness answered Mem's call. He took a step closer to me. I felt the blood pulse through my temples and then drain from my face.

What had Millie discovered that silenced her so completely? What were Mem and I about to find?

A yap from around the far corner of the house disrupted my panic. Mem dashed toward the sound. I followed close behind, turning the corner of the house right as Mem froze. Ten feet in front of us, Mr. Boots lay on the grass with one leg tucked under him at a strange angle. Millie was licking his face furiously, and he rested a shaking hand on her side.

"Chip!" Mem shouted, kneeling at his side.

Mr. Boots lifted his head a couple of inches to see him. "Remember? How did you—?"

"Millie came and got us."

"Well, I'll be," he smiled weakly and touched Millie's muzzle.

"Chip, why are you lying down out here? If you're tired, you should go to bed."

"I'm not taking a nap. I tripped over that darned thing," he said, pointing to the hose that was attached to the yard sprinkler. "I don't know if my leg's broken, but I sure as heck can't get up."

"Mem, you wait here with Mr. Boots," I said. "I'll go inside and call for help."

"I don't think there's anyone inside to call," Mem said. "Let's call right here. Help! Help! Somebody help!" *Poor Mem.*

I ran into Mr. Boots' house—for the first time ever—found his phone on a pile of newspapers, and called 911 for the second time in my life.

Mr. Boots winced in pain as the paramedics lifted him onto the stretcher and up into the ambulance. Millie growled savagely at the two uniformed men who, for all she knew, were kidnapping her master. It took both Mem and me to pull her, yanking and yelping, into the house. I could still hear her barking as we climbed into the back of the ambulance and sat on the bench alongside one of the paramedics.

The driver didn't use the siren or any extra speed, so the ride to University Hospital in Burlington took almost an hour. Mr. Boots tried to make chitchat for the first few miles, but the effort tired him, and he closed his eyes. One of the paramedics, a heavyset, suntanned man, gave him an extra blanket, and Mem gave him the weather report.

Mem was surprisingly unruffled the whole way up there. Maybe because he was with his best friend. Maybe because he likes car rides. Or maybe because he didn't really know what was going on. I seemed to be the only nervous one in the group. I couldn't help it. The sterile, too-bright lights and all the emergency equipment inside the ambulance gave me the creeps. At one point, the paramedic had to take off Mr. Boots' shoe because his foot was swelling up so much. The sight of it made me queasy. Plus, I had no idea how Mem and I were going to get ourselves back to Hull. I wished I could fast-forward through the day and find out how it all ended.

Three hours, two Dr. Peppers and a phone call later, Mr. Boots was on his way into surgery for a broken leg. Since Aunt Collette was stuck at work, Leesha and her Aunt Holly were on their way to meet us at the hospital. By the time Leesha and Holly found us in the waiting area, I'd calmed down a lot.

"How you boys holding up?" Holly asked, taking a seat on the waiting room bench.

"All right," I said.

"All right," Mem yawned.

"And Mr. Boots?"

"A doctor came by a few minutes ago and told us it's a simple fracture, whatever that means," I said.

"Gotta be better than a complicated one," Leesha noted.

"Do you have any coins for the candy machine?" Mem asked.

"Sure," Leesha said. "C'mon, Mem, you lead the way."

After an hour or so, another doctor, this one wearing green scrubs, a paper hat and clogs, appeared in the waiting room. "Are you the family of Chetwin Boots?" she asked.

"We're his friends," Holly answered. "He doesn't have family."

"I'm Dr. Gold, his surgeon." She pulled off her cap, letting a brown braid fall down her back. "Mr. Boots is in the recovery room—still groggy, but doing fine. He'll just need an overnight or two for observation and pain control."

"So he can go home tomorrow?" Mem asked. "Can we pick him up tomorrow?"

"It's not quite that simple," Dr. Gold said, turning to Holly. "I can't send him home if he's going to be alone. He'll be in a cast for six to eight weeks, and at his age, he's going to need help negotiating stairs and bathrooms, and he says he has a dog. I don't want him tripping over any animals. I'd like to send him to a nursing home for his recuperation."

"Nursing home?" Mem blurted. "But Chip will die there!"

Dr. Gold made a small smile. "I have a very nice nursing home in mind. You don't have to worry— "

"No!" he howled. "Chip told me so himself. He said a nursing home would kill him, just like it did Imogene. Right, Johnny? He'll die in a nursing home!"

"Mem," I said, "I think he was exaggerating. He didn't mean he'd actually die."

"He did mean it!" Mem's eyes were getting wet. He stepped closer to Leesha, and she patted his back. "He'll die there! I know it! He'll die!"

"Look, I know this is hard," Dr. Gold said. "Home is the best place to get better—but only if it's safe. And right now, it's not."

"I don't care! I don't care one little bit!" Mem yelled. Then his voice turned to a choked whisper. "I don't care. I don't care. I don't care. No nursing home. I don't care."

"Why don't you all get some rest tonight?" the doctor said. "You can see Mr. Boots tomorrow— visiting hours start at ten. I'll be making rounds in the late morning, and I'll explain all about the nursing home to him then."

"Good idea," said Holly before Mem could say anything more. "Thank you."

A voice came over the loudspeaker: "Dr. Gold, Dr. Debra Gold, please call extension 34."

"That's my next case," she said. "Now don't worry. No one likes the idea of a nursing home when they first hear about it, but he'll come around." With that, she hurried down the hall and disappeared into the elevator.

"He won't come around," Mem said to his feet. "He'll die. He'll just die."

"Stop that, Mem," Holly said. "He's going to be just fine. Now come on, let's go home. I'm exhausted."

We all crowded into Holly's car—Holly and me in front, Mem and Leesha in back—and got on the road toward Hull. Holly had a Beatles CD on, and for a while I zoned out on the music. I didn't feel like making conversation, and, from the look on Mem's face, he didn't, either.

"Hey Mem, guess what," Holly said after a while.

"What?"

"Before we came to pick you up, your mom had me bring Millie to your house. She's there now."

Mem looked confused. "My house? Millie?"

"She needs someplace to stay. It's not like she can fill her own food dish and let herself out in the morning—although she is a smart one, isn't she? Getting you when Mr. Boots needed your help and all."

"She loves Chip more than anything," Mem said.

Holly sighed. "I sure do hate to see that old dog and that old man separated."

"Don't worry," Leesha said. It was the first

time she'd spoken since we'd gotten in the car. "They're not going to be separated."

"But they don't allow pets in nursing homes," Holly said.

"He's not going to a nursing home." She said it like she knew it for a fact.

Holly squinted at Leesha in the rearview mirror, then glanced over at Mem. "We've got to be realistic here, Leesha. We all need to be realistic."

"I am being realistic. All we have to do is manage the system." She smiled a funny kind of smile at Mem. "Anyway, I'm starving. Can we stop at that Dairy Queen up there?"

"Hello?" I said, picking up the phone in the kitchen. We'd only been home from the hospital for ten minutes. I figured it was Aunt Collette checking in on us.

"It's Leesha."

"Oh, hey."

"Is Mem there?"

"Yup. Mem, it's for you," I called into the living room.

Mem was watching *Jeopardy* with Millie, but he came running in when I told him who was calling. "Hi, Leesha!" he hollered into the receiver. Whatever she said to him then, it made him glance up at me suspiciously and turn his back before answering. "Okay, all right," he said in a loud whisper. "Yup… nope…I promise, honest…when?…yup…okay, bye." He hung up, took another wary look at me, and rushed back to the TV.

Something was up. Definitely. Obviously.

The phone rang again a minute later. This time, it had to be Aunt Collette. "Hi," I said.

"Johnny?" said Jo.

Jo—oh, no! I'd totally forgotten our lunch plans at Niko's! "Jo, I'm sorry— "

"Did you forget? Again?" Her voice was a knife.

"No—I mean, yes. I mean…Mr. Boots got hurt, and Mem and I had to— "

"Who?"

"Mr. Boots. The old guy who lives next door to me. He tripped in the yard and broke his leg. I had to go to the hospital with him."

"Why—are you related?"

"He doesn't have any relatives. He's a friend."

"Oh. Well, you could've called to let me know."

"I should've."

"Yeah, you should've. We had plans."

"I'm sorry."

"I'm not gonna keep giving you chances."

"I know, I know. Just one more chance, please? Tomorrow. Let's do tomorrow."

"I don't know. What did you have in mind?"

"We could...um...well..."

She exhaled loudly. "Okay, look. I'm getting my sports physical first thing in the morning, and then my mom and I are going out to breakfast. I can have her drop me off at the Fort River bridge after that—I'll bring my tube. Let's make it eleven."

"O-okay, but I've got Mem till three. I'm not supposed to leave him alone for long."

"Fine, whatever. Just be there."

"We'll be there."

"Eleven sharp, Johnny. I'm not waiting around."

"You won't have to. Tubing at eleven. See ya."

"See ya."

When I hung up, I didn't know whether to feel like a Romeo or a scolded puppy. But it didn't really matter. What mattered was that Jo had agreed to see me. Tubing down the river with the beautiful Josephine. Eleven o'clock tomorrow morning. I'd be there by 10:30. And even though Mem would be there too, I knew it would still feel like a date.

Chapter 15

On her way out the next morning, Aunt Collette said she'd probably be late getting home, in which case we'd have to put off visiting Mr. Boots until the next day. That was rotten luck, but at least I wouldn't have to rush home from my date with Jo.

Once Aunt Collette backed out of the driveway, I let Millie run around the yard and then fed her some leftover spaghetti. As I was scrounging around the kitchen for my own breakfast, the phone rang, and Mem flew in to pick it up. He cupped his hand around his mouth and the receiver, as if that was going to stop me from overhearing. "Hello?" he said. "Uh huh...yeah, I know where it is...okay, if you're sure...all right...I said I promise...okay..." So he and Leesha were still scheming. Fine—I didn't care. In less than an hour,

Mem and I would be on our way to meet Jo. I found a bag of popcorn in the pantry and took it to the kitchen table while they conspired.

When Mem finally hung up, he marched to the table and plunked down in the chair opposite me. "We gotta go to the bus," he said.

"What?"

"The bus, Johnny, the bus station. Leesha's gonna be there at ten."

I pushed the popcorn away and sat back. "Why? Is she expecting someone?"

"Just us. We gotta catch the 10:15 to Burlington. To see Chip."

"No way, Mem. We're not going to Burlington this morning. We're going tubing this morning. Aunt Collette will take us to see Chip tomorrow."

"No!" he pounded his fist on the table, but he looked more excited than mad. "We have to go this morning, and we have to go with Leesha. It's the only way, Johnny."

"The only way for what?"

"The only way to save Chip's life."

"His life isn't in danger, Mem."

"Yes, it is."

"Well, if Leesha thinks she can save him, let her do it herself. I'm not cancelling out on Jo again."

"Huh?"

"She's meeting us at the bridge at eleven. You want to see Jo, don't you?"

"You want to see Jo, don't you? C'mon, Johnny, we got to do this—for Chip. Just tell Jo to meet us later. Or tomorrow."

"I can't. She's out and she doesn't have a cell. Besides, what does Leesha think she's gonna do that can't wait?"

"I told you, she's gonna save Chip's life." He looked up at the wall clock, and so did I. It was almost 9:45. "Johnny, let's go." His voice climbed an octave. "Please. Please please please please!"

But I wasn't giving in. "Look, Mem. Leesha's a big girl. She can take the bus by herself if she wants to go so badly. She doesn't need us."

"She does! She needs me."

"Why?"

"I'm her ambassador. Whatever that means."

"Well, she'll have to find another ambassador because I can't come."

"Then I'll go without you. Leesha will take care of me."

"Not a chance, Mem. My life would be in danger if Aunt Collette found out. We're supposed to stick together. You know that."

"Then just come. Come on, Johnny, don't worry."

"I'm not worried. I'm just not going."

Mem hung his head, and when he lifted it back up, his big owl eyes were moist. "In school we learned that people help their friends."

"I know, but— "

"We learned that people trust their friends."

"C'mon, Mem."

"I thought we were friends, you and me," he said.

"We are."

"I thought you and me and Leesha and Chip were all friends."

"Mem, we are."

"We should trust Leesha. We should help Chip. We should go."

I thought about how Mem rescued me the day Dirk tried to pound me. How he taught me his video game maneuvers and then taught my friends. I thought about how much harder Mem's life was than mine—how much harder it would always be. How he almost never asked for anything because he liked his summer just the way it was. And now here he was, asking me for this one thing—this one thing that wasn't even for himself, but for a broken-legged old man in the hospital.

"No," I said. "I'm not going."

He wiped his eyes and pushed his chair back so hard, it fell over. "Well, I am!"

"Mem, you can't. You can't go anywhere without me."

"Watch me!" he said, and then he ran out of the room.

"Mem, stop," I yelled, but when I got to the living room, he was already out the front door. Great, just perfect. If I let Mem try to go to the bus station by himself, he'd end up leaping into traffic or mutilating himself with broken glass or something. And even if he somehow managed to get as far as the station, Leesha wouldn't know how to handle him on her own, no way. I sprinted after him without bothering to put shoes on.

Mem had reached the street by the time I caught up with him. "You can't do this," I said, grabbing his arm, but he was stronger than I realized, and he pulled away.

"Yes, I can!" he said, walking fast. "I can. Because I'm a good friend, that's why."

"I'll call Aunt Collette."

That stopped him dead. "You're gonna squeal on me, Johnny? You're really gonna?"

"That's right." I glanced at his big grey eyes but had to look away. "I mean, listen..." I stood up taller. "Look, Mem…" I coughed and rubbed my forehead, and then I sighed a sigh from the very pit of my gut. There was no way I was going to win this fight. The sooner I admitted defeat, the sooner we could get on with it. "You know," I said, "Jo is never gonna speak to me again."

He gazed at me solemnly. "Did she lose her voice?"

"No, she's just gonna be that mad at me."

"Oh. I like Jo. She's pretty."

"Yeah, well anyway, I'm barefoot. Hold on while I get my flip flops."

Leesha seemed surprised to see me. I guess Mem didn't mention how we were as good as handcuffed together this summer. When I told her I sacrificed my day, my summer, my big chance with Jo for this scheme, she said thanks and sorry and it'll be worth it, but she still wouldn't tell me what it was all about. "I can't, not in front of Mem," she whispered. "He'll be too upset if it bombs. You know, like Monopoly upset or me moving back to Chicago upset. Later, though. Honest."

Great.

The bus dropped us off right in front of the hospital. We piled out, along with a few other people, and went straight to the surgical ward on the third floor. Mr. Boots had a room to himself down at the far end of the hall. When we got there, he was sitting up in bed, eating Jell-O and fiddling with the TV remote.

"Chip!" Mem gushed from the doorway. "Chip, it's me. And this is my friend Leesha. She's my new friend. My friend and Johnny's friend too."

"Well, I'll be," he said, stopping his spoon midair. "Come inside, all of you," he waved with a hand attached to some sort of monitor. He looked good, considering he'd just had an operation. He needed a shave, and the hospital-issue pajamas didn't do much for him, but he looked pretty much his usual self.

"Hi, Mr. Boots," I said, trying to ignore the smell—like powdered eggs mixed with Lysol.

"Have a seat, why don't you?" he said.

Mem sat down at the foot of the bed, and Leesha took the chair next to the IV pole. I was heading for the recliner in the corner when Leesha said, "Um, Johnny? I need to talk to Mr. Boots."

"Go ahead."

"Privately."

Wait a minute—did she really drag me all the way to Burlington just to throw me out? I took one look at her face and knew the answer.

"Please," she said.

I looked to Mr. Boots, who only shrugged and changed the channel. "Fine," I said. "Just perfect." I couldn't believe I'd blown it with Jo for this. "Mem too?"

"Mem," she said, "do you want to go with Johnny or stay here and watch The Weather Channel?" Like he was going to pass up a chance to watch Martin the Meteorologist. So it was just me being expelled. Figures.

There was a small waiting room at the other end of the hall, so I holed myself up in there. For a full half-hour, I paged through the magazines on the coffee table and watched the nurses walk past, their rubber-soled shoes squeaking against the linoleum. The last time I looked up, Dr. Gold was walking by. She was probably on her way to check on Mr. Boots and give him The Talk, I figured. Not good. Mem was bound to get unstrung all over again if he had to hear that speech, and I wouldn't be in the room to talk him down. Well, I'd probably hear him howling all the way from here, so I could run down there if I needed to.

Twenty minutes later, Leesha and Mem came to get me. Leesha offered no explanations or sorries. She just said, "We can go now," so we did. We caught the 1:10 bus and spent the whole ride in silence, with Mem drifting off, Leesha smiling faintly to herself, and me picturing a whole long summer without Jo. When we got off at Hull, Leesha mouthed to me, "Later. Promise." Like that was supposed to make everything all right. Like that meant I wouldn't be miserable anymore.

There's not much to say about the rest of the day. Jo wouldn't take my calls—surprise, surprise. I tried four times until her mom finally said, "Look, Johnny, I don't know what's going on, but maybe you should give it some time." I asked her if she thought time might actually help. She didn't say anything, but she didn't need to. The answer was crystal clear: I'd lost Jo forever.

When Mom called to say hi, she was all excited about paint chips and fabric swatches and floor tiles. I tried to sound enthusiastic, but I must not have done a very good job of faking it because she said I sounded a little hoarse and wanted to know if I felt all right. I told her it must be a bad connection because I was fine.

That night, I went to bed earlier than I had all summer, which made Aunt Collette worry that I was sick too, but the truth was, I just wanted this day to be over. I didn't even care what Leesha's big mystery was anymore. It's not like it could bring Jo back to me. Nothing could do that. When it's over, it's over—I learned that when my parents got divorced. And while my dad might have turned around and met Kim a heartbeat later, I knew I was never going to get over Jo. Never.

That's what I was thinking about when Mem tiptoed into my room, followed closely by Millie. I was lying in bed listening to my iPod. It was almost 11:30.

"What?" I said, pulling my headphones off.

"Phone. For you. She says, I don't know, she wants to talk it over."

I jumped up and seized the phone, motioning Mem out of the room. I couldn't believe she was going to give me another chance. This was too good to have hoped for. "Jo?"

"Leesha."

"Oh." I dropped onto the bed. How stupid could I get?

"Try to contain your enthusiasm."

"I just thought..."

"I know what you thought. Look, I need some help."

"I think I'm all done helping, Leesha. I'm tired."

Silence. Some static. A throat-clearing. Then, "Johnny, I'm desperate. I wouldn't be bothering you except that it's crucial. I really, really need help."

I rubbed my face and fell belly-up on the bed. Millie jumped up and curled herself into a ball next to me. "What kind of help?"

"The kind for managing the system."

"Is it legal?"

"Of course it's legal. I'll explain everything, like I promised. But first can I tell you what I need or not?"

"Might as well," I said. It wasn't like I had anything else going on.

Chapter 16

"Hey guys," Aunt Collette said. "Help TJ move the television into the sitting room, would you? I'm going to rig up a footstool." It was two days after our bus trip to Burlington, and we were getting Mr. Boots' place ready for his return home.

"You ever been inside here?" I asked Mem as we headed to Chip's bedroom, Millie at our heels.

"Uh-uh. But it's just like your side." He was right, sort of. The rooms were the same shape and size as my side of the duplex, but Mr. Boots' stuff was so different—older, darker, dusty-smelling— you felt like you were in a different century.

"Believe it or not, I was only in here once," I said, "when I ran in to call the ambulance the other day."

"But you live right here," Mem said.

"I know."

"And you're friends."

"Yeah, well..."

"Okay, boys," said TJ in his yellow Hawaiian shirt. He unplugged the TV, a hulking, old-fashioned one that took over the entire top of Mr. Boots' dresser. "This is going to take all three of us. Johnny, you take one side. I'll take the other. And Mem, you direct us into the living room, all right?"

The trip to the living room went pretty smoothly, except for when we almost got stuck in the doorway. And when Mem tripped over Millie. And when I backed into the grandfather clock. Anyway, we made it. TJ and I set the TV on the coffee table, which Aunt Collette had pushed against the wall opposite the couch. She already had the sofa set up with extra pillows, the remote, three days' worth of unread newspapers, a tray on wheels, and a milk-crate footstool.

"Looks great," TJ said, surveying the room we'd designated as Recovery Headquarters.

"Not bad," Aunt Collette agreed.

I watched the two of them, trying to get used to the idea of them as a couple, imagining them being a family one day. Okay, so it was a little early to start ringing the wedding bells, but at least they had a shot now. Last night, we all went to talk to Mr. Dempster about the golf course and the zoning change. Aunt Collette, TJ, Mem and I showed up at the Dempsters' door right after supper, and *hallelujah*, Mr. Dempster was in a decent mood, and he said it sounded like a pretty good idea. Something about how it would bring people and their money to town. So I hadn't screwed it up for them. Maybe I'd screwed things up for Jo and me, but Aunt Collette and TJ still had a fighting chance.

"Johnny, when is Mo supposed to get here with the gas?" Aunt Collette asked. "I want to get the lawn mowed before Chip arrives."

"He's getting a ride from his mom. I'll give him a call, see where they're at." As I headed toward the kitchen though, a car pulled into the driveway. "That must be Mo now." The car honked, and Millie ran to the front door, woofing.

"Quiet, Millie," Aunt Collette hushed.

"She just wants to say hi," Mem said. "C'mon, girl, let's go see." He opened the door, and she barreled down the front steps. Only, it wasn't Mo pulling in. It was Leesha and Holly delivering Mr. Boots! We all ran outside.

Mr. Boots was half-sitting, half-lying in the back seat with his casted leg propped on the center console. He looked a little worn out, and his face was thinner than before, but he was all smiles just the same. When Leesha opened the door for him, Millie jumped right in. You'd think she hadn't seen her master in a year, the way she was yelping and running in circles on the car seat.

"Hi, Chip!" Mem crowed. "Hi! Bet you're glad to be home, huh? Bet you're glad we helped you get home!"

"Okay, all right, little missy," he told Millie, who was now covering his face in kisses. "You bet I am, Mem. Let's get inside already."

Holly got his crutches out of the car, and we all escorted him inside—all of us except Leesha, who was rummaging for something in the trunk. The front steps were slow going, but TJ gave Mr. Boots a hand, and it was okay.

"Well, will you look at this?" Mr. Boots said once he stepped inside, panting a little from the stair-climbing. "You've set me up so I never have to leave the couch."

"Just while you're getting better," Aunt Collette said. "Now, let's get you comfortable, and then I'll fix some lunch, how's that?"

"Doubt there's anything fresh in the 'fridge. How about we order some pizza, my treat?"

"Pizza my treat! Pizza my treat! Hooray!" shouted Mem. "I'm starving. How about you, Johnny? How about you, Leesha...Leesha?"

"Coming," she called from the front porch. She walked in, carrying a big black bag on each shoulder. "Heavy objects coming through. Somebody show me where."

"I will," I said, taking one of the bags from her.

"Me too," Mem chimed.

The three of us went into the spare bedroom— the bedroom that was just like mine, kind of. Same shape, same double window, but it was off-white instead of green, it had an old-fashioned quilt on the bed instead of a down comforter, and there were no band posters taped to the walls. Leesha dropped her shoulder bag onto the bed, and I set the other one next to it.

"So?" I asked.

"It's fine," she said, glancing around. "Could be better, could be a lot worse. I won't be in here much anyway. I'll be way too busy."

"Tell us again," Mem urged. "Tell us what you are now, Leesha."

"I am..." she gleamed. "I am Chip Boots'

professional companion-slash-assistant. I am a Hull resident for the whole summer. The occupant of this fine bedroom. The person who's going to cut Chip's hair this afternoon. The girl who doesn't have to go back to Chicago tomorrow. The one who's going to hang out with the two of you until September."

"Hooray!" shouted Mem. "Hooray for the whole summer! Hooray for miracles!"

For a terrifying moment, I thought we were going to have to do a group hug. Leesha put both arms out, and Mem started leaning in—but I was saved by the bell. The doorbell, that is. Finally, Mo. "That's for me," I said and hurried out of the room.

"Come in, Mo," I heard Aunt Collette say. "Leave that can outside though. Millie, you stay here."

"Hey," I said. "Thanks for the gas."

"Sure," Mo said.

"Want to hang for a while? We're ordering pizza."

"You don't have to."

"It's no problem."

"No, I mean you really don't have to," he said nodding toward the front door.

I didn't know what he was talking about, but I took his cue and stepped out onto the front steps. Mo's mother was still parked in the driveway, and someone was getting out of the passenger side. It was Jo, carrying three big boxes of pizza! I hadn't seen or talked to her since I blew our bridge date. She looked beautiful in her white sundress. I ran down to meet her while her mom backed out and drove away.

"Hey," she said, handing me the still-hot boxes.

"Hey."

"I thought you might be hungry."

"Thanks. Um, yeah, thanks. I...do you want to come in?"

She gazed down at her feet and then up at the house. "Mo told me what happened the day we were supposed to go tubing. What you were doing for the old guy."

"I'm sorry, Jo. I really should have— "

"No, let me talk. I'm the one who's sorry. You were doing a good thing, and you didn't have a choice, and I should've..." Finally, she looked me in the eye. "I should've..."

I was smiling now. "You know what? I'm starving."

Jo looked incredibly relieved. "Me too. Let's eat."

As we turned to head inside, I suddenly felt like I was floating above the rooftop, looking down. I saw Jo and me on the driveway, Mem and Leesha in her room, Mr. Boots and Millie on the couch, Aunt Collette and TJ in the kitchen. Funny how the summer that started out in the pits had turned into something so exceptional. And none of it would have been possible without Mem. Granted, I didn't know what was going to happen down the road with Jo and me, or with Aunt Collette and TJ, or with Leesha and her family problems. But I did know one thing: Mem and I were always going to be more than cousins. We were going to be friends.

As I looked down at Jo and me one last time, I wondered what kind of pizza was in the boxes. But it didn't really matter. It was going to be perfect, even if it had tofu on top. As perfect as blue skies and starry nights.

SHIRLEY REVA VERNICK'S interviews and feature articles have appeared in *Cosmopolitan, Salon, Good Housekeeping, Ladies' Home Journal,* national newspapers and the publications of Harvard, Johns Hopkins and Boston Universities. She also runs a popular storytelling website, storybee.org, which is used in schools, libraries, hospitals and homes all over the world. She lives in Amherst, Massachusetts.

In 2012, her debut novel, *The Blood Lie,* was listed on the American Library Association's list for Best Fiction for Young Adults. It received the Simon Wiesenthal Once Upon a World Children's Book Award and was an Honor Book for both the Sydney Taylor Book Award and the Skipping Stones Award.